The Art of Falling in Love with Your Grumpy Neighbor

ANNE KEMP

This book is for anyone out there who has ever had to deal with someone (a neighbor, perhaps?) who tries to steal your joy.

Don't let them.
Be the bright light and just keep shining.

xoxo

ONE

Austin

The relentless banging on my front door is like a bad drum solo—one that makes you want to bash your head against a wall. It's not like it's been going on for hours, but it's hit that sweet spot where my patience is officially on vacation. Long enough that I'm considering a dramatic dive through the window to escape it, but short enough that I know it's not a random delivery guy. This isn't a "Here's your Amazon package" knock. Not out here in the middle of nowhere.

No, this knock screams "family." Specifically, one annoyingly persistent brother who's like a dog with a bone.

"Hey!"

The voice floats through the house, and I freeze. There's no one here, right? Except... it sounds exactly like Levi. My brother. But I definitely didn't let him in, and I know he doesn't have a key.

I inch toward the foyer, eyes narrowing at the mail slot in the door. The metal lip jiggles, then lifts like it's possessed by a very determined ghost.

"Austin! Yo, Austin!" Levi's voice booms through the slot.

1

"Austin Porter!"

Why anyone thought a mail slot in a door was necessary on a farm in the middle of nowhere is beyond me. We've got a mailbox. But Grandma insisted on one, probably just to confuse the mailman.

With an eye roll that could power a wind turbine, I yank the door open. The look on Levi's face is worth every second of my irritation. He's hunched over like a gargoyle, hand cupped around his mouth, ready to unleash another shout through the slot.

"What do you want?" I snap, shoving a hand through my hair. Levi, of all people, should know that when I say I want to be left alone, I mean it. And I literally told him that last night on the phone.

Levi scrambles to his feet, grabbing at a brown paper bag and a beverage container on the porch. "I've got croissants and coffee for us. Can I come in?"

I don't bother to respond; he won't listen if I say no. Instead, I simply walk away from the door, leaving it open to his interpretation, and head back into the living room where I drop into my old recliner.

A large bay window dominates one side of the room, offering a breathtaking view of a picturesque pond. The water shimmers in the light, reflecting the greenery of the surrounding landscape. Just beyond the pond is a neat boxwood hedge, and on the other side, a neighboring house stands with a moving truck parked out front—a truck that's been there for at least a day, hinting at the recent arrival.

"Your new neighbor is moving in today," Levi says as he puts the coffee on a table beside me and hands me a croissant. His eyes dance across the tabletop, taking in a set of binoculars I left parked there. "Obviously, you saw, too. Are you going to walk over and say hello or stare at them through your weirdo goggles like a homicidal maniac?"

When I cut my eyes his way, he watches me with an expression on his face that reminds me of one of our mother's cherub statues. Levi the angel.

"You know..." I sigh, holding the mug to my lips. "I wasn't asked by the welcoming committee to go by, so..."

"Like there's a welcoming committee that would have you as a member." Levi chuckles, his eyes rocking to the television that's powered off for once. He nods toward it. "If I pull up YouTube, what's your search history going to look like?"

Gripping my cardboard takeaway coffee cup, I take a deep breath in and focus on not crushing it before I slowly let the air out, counting to eight. Bless therapy, I've actually come a long way since my accident.

I stare at Levi pointedly. "I don't need you policing what I choose to watch."

"When you're rewatching the moment you were injured on the field, yes," he says with a shrug. "Yes, you do."

"Did you come over to chastise me this morning?" I try to keep the sarcasm out of my voice, but it seeps from my pores.

Levi studies me with a furrowed brow. "I'm worried about you. You spend a lot of time out here, watching football, alone. You know that makes you seem a little cuckoo, right?"

"If by cuckoo you mean invested in my healing process, then okay." I tip my coffee cup in the air, toasting Levi. "Here's to me being the cuckooiest of all the cuckoo birds there are."

Do I want to admit that I sometimes sit here and question if I'll ever go back to the NFL? That I replay the moment I went down on the field, in my mind, day and night like watching and rewatching a trending video again and again on TikTok?

No. I don't.

"Cuckooiest," Levi repeats. "That's not a word. And you know I'm right. You hardly leave this place, if ever."

"I get social company from Amy."

"Your housekeeper?" Levi cocks his head to the side. "You told me she was always hitting on you. When she started, your underwear went missing. I thought you were getting rid of her?"

"Like I'm going to take the time to find a new one?" I snap back. So the maid keeps hitting on me and I find it highly uncomfortable and inappropriate. As a semi-reclusive soul, I'm not in the position to pick and choose my helpers at the moment. "And, I do leave the house. I do things like run errands and go to therapy."

"Your therapist comes here—and it's not just about that." Levi crosses his arms in front of his chest as he leans back in his seat. "I was just in town visiting our tenants at the apartment buildings. We have four buildings now, and all with tenants who have different needs. One of those needs is being able to get in touch with someone, namely one of us, when they have an issue."

Honestly. This again? "They've got our numbers, right?"

"They do, but it doesn't work if you don't pick up the phone." Levi stares at me intensely. "Did you know that Pearl had a small kitchen fire about a week ago?"

"What?" This news makes me sit up taller. Pearl is one of our older tenants, who also happened to be a very good friend to my grandparents.

"She tried to call, but you didn't answer, so she called me. Luckily I was here, in town, and not out on the road with the team. I was originally supposed to be away coaching that week."

"Lucky us." I can't help that the words come out a bit snarkier than planned, but they do. Of course, there's a minute amount of sarcasm dripping from each word. My brother—also known as Midas, the one who was king of the NFL—he didn't have to step back and consider retirement because of an Achilles injury. No. He stepped back on his merit so he could slow down, start a family, and then segue into coaching.

How *perfect* for him.

"Honestly." Levi sighs. "You don't need to be so cranky all the time. You know, when Mom comes to visit you, I can tell by the sound of her voice. She always calls me after and needs a pick-me-up."

A tiny stab pierces my icy heart. "I drag her down that much?"

"You've been a spiteful human for the last year." Levi stands up, shaking his finger my way, like a parent dealing with a petulant child. "All through your therapy, they've been telling you to work on your head and mindset…but no. You sit here and go through the motions."

This is not the way I envisioned my morning when I woke up, let me tell you. "If you only stopped by to give me grief, Levi, you need to go. It's Saturday and I have things I need to do."

"Austin, it's Sunday." Levi sighs and hangs his head. "This is exactly why I'm worried about you. You're sitting in the dark, alone as usual, with a pair of binoculars, doing what?"

"Well, today, I'm being lectured by my brother," I say as I cross my arms in front of me, trying to build my own wall between us.

"I don't want to lecture you, but I'm worried. We're worried."

"By we you mean…?"

"Me and Mom." He pauses. "Since you lost out on buying that house, you've been a little unhinged."

That's news to me. "How?"

"Look, I'm glad you're living in our grandparents' old house," he continues, ignoring my question. "It's good you're here so you can concentrate on your recovery—"

I interrupt him with a loud snort. Good on him, though, cause he keeps going.

"—and to focus on you. But you've got to get some life back. You ain't dead yet, you're injured."

There's a bit of irritation igniting inside me. The kind that's only reserved for family members. Bless 'em. They take the brunt sometimes, don't they? Well-meaning, they are. They want to share their sage advice, life experiences, and all that jazz. But come on. Do it if I ask, okay? Don't offer it up to me like you're doing me a service.

"I think you should go." I incline my head toward the main hallway. "Don't let the door hit you in the butt on the way out. Y'all come back now...ya here? And bless your heart."

"Did you just triple Southern-woman-goodbye me out the door?" Levi asks, gasping in faux surprise.

"I did. Keep it up and I may help toss you out if you won't go on your own accord."

"I don't know what's crawled up your butt lately," Levi says, shaking his head like he's diagnosing a patient, then he glances across the paddock to the house again before turning back to me. "But I sure pity your new neighbor."

The only comeback I can muster is slamming the door as he heads down the steps. In my mind, I picture it with enough force that Levi is blasted by an invisible shockwave, sending him somersaulting across the yard like a cartoon character until he lands in a heap by his car—or better yet, flipping head over heels all the way to the main road.

Honestly, I don't know what's crawled up my butt lately either, but I do know it feels damn good to be alone. Completely alone, out here in the country, with no one to bother me.

Now, I just have to make sure the new neighbor understands that sooner rather than later.

TWO

Dex

Moving. It's like signing up for a stress marathon, right up there in the top ten life stressors, sandwiched between "death of a loved one" and "saying 'I do'"—and that's not even in the right order.

I glance around at the mountain of boxes cluttering the living room, and a part of me wants to scream. That's the drama queen side of me—the one that's convinced calm is a mythical creature. She's done with the chaos and was hoping to hit the reset button here in Sweetkiss Creek. But let's face it, she's not as good at handling stress as she used to be.

"We're done, ma'am," the mover says as he stands in my doorway. "All of your boxes are in the rooms according to what was written on the outside of them. Truck is empty."

"Thank you," I say, rising from the spot by the couch where I've been busy digging through a container looking for my hair dryer. Because, of course, I remember packing it with my living room things. "You guys were the best. That was a big trip from California to North Carolina."

"Lucky for me, though," he says, nodding his head out toward the road that runs outside my property. "My grandparents live about an hour away in Asheville. Headed there now for a few days' respite."

Now there's someone who looks at the brighter side of things. Smiling, I watch as he jogs over to the truck, joining the other two men who're waiting in the cab. With a final wave, he hops behind the wheel and pulls away.

Leaving me alone, for the first time, in my house. MY house. MY FIRST HOUSE!

I take a giant leap from the front door into the foyer. In my mind, I am a graceful prima ballerina, one who has performed on all of the stages around the world to large audiences, receiving accolades and standing ovations wherever I go. However, I'm aware that if someone was filming this, I'd come across more "past-my-prima" than lithe dancer.

But that's okay. No one is around to see me, are they? Cause I'm in *MY HOUSE!*

Giggling with no self-control, I wrap my arms around my torso and spin in a circle. Look, I've lived in Los Angeles for a long time. Getting the chance to own my own home, thanks to my best friend, and to move away from the city and a life filled with stressors, is pretty exciting.

I pull my phone from my back pocket and, tapping the app I was looking for, press start to kick my playlist off. The fortune that Bruno Mars's "Uptown Funk" is the first song to play does not escape me. I like it. It's an eight out of ten on the butt-shaking scale, at least for me.

I start moving around the place, dancing from room to room. I love this house so much. When you walk into the modest two-story home, you're greeted by a small foyer that's basically going to be a drop zone for boots, coats, and the occasional forgotten grocery bag. There's a wooden bench that's seen better days, but it'll do the job—mostly holding a pile of my mismatched shoes, but it's a job nonetheless.

To the right is the living room, where my old couch and a

couple of armchairs have set up camp around an old fireplace. That fireplace is the true MVP of the house; I can already see it working overtime in the winter and making the place feel like a cozy retreat. The brick hearth gives it that "I totally have my life together" vibe, even if the rest of the room says otherwise. Built-in shelves along one wall will soon be blessed with books I swear I'll read someday, and I'll add a few family photos and knick-knacks...they seem to multiply when I'm not looking. A big window lets in plenty of sunlight—and I can't wait to sit in its warmth and read on my first quiet weekend.

The kitchen is a no-nonsense space with painted wooden cabinets that could use a fresh coat but haven't bothered to ask for one, and the back door leads to a porch that's perfect for sunset watching—or pretending I'm on top of all those DIY projects I'm planning on tackling.

The master bedroom upstairs is small and cozy, but complete with its own bathroom, and the other bedrooms are just as modest—basically enough room for a bed, a dresser, and a lot of wishful thinking.

All in all, my house is a mix of cozy charm and mild chaos —kind of like me. It's not perfect, but it's home, and that's good enough for now.

My eyes closed, I make sure to belt out the words, singing nice and loud. I'm in the middle of a giant spin when I turn around and open my eyes to find a familiar face standing in the front doorway with a large basket in her arms.

"WHAT THE...!!" My scream is loud and long and I'm pretty sure I do a whole jogging and tap dance routine while standing in place.

"Sorry!" The visitor cackles as she puts the basket on the nearest cardboard box and covers her mouth with her hand in a sad attempt to hide her amusement from me. "In my defense, the door was wide open."

"I was busy dancing," I say, waving my hand in the direction of the door as I turn down the volume on my phone. "Couldn't really close the door now, could I?" Slowing my breath down, I stop and cock my head to the side, smiling at my friend. "It's so good to see you Georgie!"

"Bex Madden!" With a little squeal she runs to me and throws her arms around me. "Welcome to Sweetkiss Creek. I am still in shock that you're here now. Who would have thought it could be this easy?"

"I wouldn't call moving easy," I say with a snicker, wagging my finger in the air. "One thing for sure, this is a lesson in patience. If the journey so far had its own soundtrack, let's just say the song 'Life Is a Highway' would for sure be on there."

Georgie frowns. "Not, 'On the Road Again'? I would have thought Willie Nelson for the win."

"Nope. No Willie on this trip, funny enough. But I didn't pick 'Highway to Hell,' did I?"

Georgie is in on the secret that I like to put a soundtrack to all the moments in my life. It's a funny habit from when I was little that has stuck with me as I've grown up and moved into an adulthood-adjacent time in my life.

"Well, you're here. I'm sure there will be more theme-song moments and memories to be made, now that you're on the East Coast." Georgie scans the room, whistling with approval. "This place is super sweet."

"Thank you," I say as I peek at the basket she'd discarded on top of a moving box. "Books! Perfect. I've got just the spot for them," I say, nodding toward the built-in bookcases in the living room that flank the fireplace. It's good to have a book-store owner as a friend, let me tell you.

"When you said you were going to need to fill some shelves, I took that as a challenge," she says with a wink. "Get ready, I've got more to bring by as soon as you say when."

"Once I have a chance to go through the boxes and see

how much space I'm actually taking up on those shelves, I will let you know."

"Amazing," Georgie coos as she claps her hands together. Turning around, she scans the room before pointing out the large bay window that faces the back of the property. "Ummm, that's a big hedge."

"I know. I like it, but only just this much," I say, holding up my hand and pinching my thumb and forefinger so they almost touch. "I appreciate boxwood hedges, but I think I want to see about removing that one."

Georgie turns to face me slowly, her eyebrows arching almost to her hairline. If I'm not mistaken, it looks as if she could be chewing on her cheek, like she's trying to stop herself from laughing.

"You want to remove the hedge?"

"Not remove as much as maybe cut into it some," I say with a flick of my wrist, indicating beyond the hedge. "There's a beautiful pond on the other side of it and I'd love to have a better view."

Georgie crosses her arms and looks at me, her eyes dancing with pure delight. "Have you spoken to your neighbor about this?"

"Not yet, but I plan on it. Although, I think that hedge is technically on my property. If that's the case, I don't need to discuss it with my neighbor, do I?"

Something in the way Georgie looks at me makes me take a pause. "Why, Georgie?"

She closes her eyes. "That hedge belongs to Austin."

That's a twist I didn't see coming. "Austin?"

She nods, opening her eyes back up wide. "Yep."

Now, there's a name with the power to make my heart skip a beat.

"How is he?"

"He's pretty much sequestered himself in that house," she

says with a shrug, her gaze wandering across the field in the direction of his property. "He's always there, going nowhere and doing nothing."

"Really?" I shake my head. Surely I didn't hear that right. "Austin?"

"He's angry now, Bex. Not the same guy. You know how they thought he had a knee injury? Turns out it was his Achilles. He's been retreating into a solo world of loneliness and bitterness for months. It's like watching a really slow train wreck."

A sadness washes over me. Angry, bitter Austin? It doesn't seem to gel with the person who I know. Or knew? "I remember he was pretty down in the dumps, or at least appeared to be, at your wedding."

Georgie nods. "He's been sliding downhill since then. We've all tried to get him to see his way out of the dark, but he seems to like it there. The other day, I had to stop by with some paperwork from Levi, and I was really surprised at how he's let himself go."

Georgie is married to Levi Porter, Austin's brother and a former NFL star himself. As chance would have it, I was in town looking for a place to live and had just met Georgie when she started dating Levi. So, by proxy, I'd gotten to know Austin some. We were the extra friends/wingman and wingwoman on dates here and there. It's fair to say I started crushing on him, and a small part of me thought he was feeling something, too.

But after his injury, he disappeared. I saw him briefly at Georgie's wedding, but we never spoke. It was like we'd never met.

Still. I am curious. "What do you mean, let himself go?"

"Austin was always the kind of guy who had his beard either trimmed or was clean shaven. He liked being pulled together. When I saw him a few days ago, he was sitting in his threadbare sweatpants on the back porch, no shirt on, hadn't shaved in weeks, probably, and he was really busy trying out his new binoculars."

There's a red-flag moment if I ever saw one coming. "Binoculars? Good to know."

"I wish I was kidding." Georgie gives me a look as she rolls her eyes. "So, don't be hanging out around here in your underwear..."

"Oh, stop it," I say, taking a playful swipe at her arm while she cracks up. "He can't be that bad."

"He's not horrible, but he's not the guy you met originally. At least he isn't right now. He's cranky, reclusive, and harmless. You don't need to worry about him—unless you want to do something about *that* hedge."

Eyeing the hedge, I shrug. "I'll see. I've got a lot on my plate. These boxes won't unpack themselves."

"What about work?" she asks.

"I'm going to figure it out. I've got some time with what I've saved, but I'll need to secure steady work soon-ish. It's going to be a bit of a mission, though."

"Because of the Graves?"

Georgie knows another little secret of mine: I have an auto-immune disease called Graves' disease. Not that I want it to be a secret. It's just...it's mine and I've been dealing with it for only a couple of years now. Graves' disease is when you have an overactive thyroid and it can cause a myriad of problems. Like many auto-immune diseases, this one is not the same for each person who has it.

"Exactly. Spencer knew me when I was diagnosed, so when he offered me the job to be his assistant, he was well aware of what I was going through. Made it a lot..."

"Simpler," Georgie finishes for me. She reaches out and squeezes my arm. "You have a good friend in Spencer."

"Right? Without his help, I would not be standing in my own home."

Spencer Stoll is not only my former employer and one of the most sought-after stars of stage and screen right now, but he's also my best friend. He and his wife, Amelia, had moved to Sweetkiss Creek a couple of years back, and after a few visits here, I too saw the heaven that they did in this little community.

Sweetkiss Creek is like something created for a Hallmark show in that it's picture-book perfect. You fall in love with the people here as much as you do with the area itself. I know I fell in love with Sweetkiss Creek and vowed to settle here. When I did, Spencer and Amelia surprised me by investing in a small house on the outskirts of town and kind of gifted it to me. By gift, I mean I don't owe the bank, I owe them, which is winning.

"Not everyone gets the chance you've gotten to move into their own house like this."

"I'm still paying for it, though," I remind her.

"True," she says as she glances at her watch. "Time is slipping away from me today. I need to get going, but I had to come see you."

"Thanks for stopping by," I say as I embrace her.

"Welcome to Sweetkiss Creek, Bex," she says as her eyes flit to the house behind mine. "Just watch out for those crazy neighbors."

Closing the door behind her, I lean against it and sigh. My muscles, which were feeling strong and ready to go a couple of hours before, are now feeling tired, worn out. Stress can make Graves rear its ugly head, so I know it's time for me to slow down soon.

Looking at the boxes in the foyer, I make a silent agreement with myself: I'll put away two of them, then call for a pizza to be delivered and spend the rest of the day relaxing.

* * *

The true measure of a good night's sleep? The puddle of drool on my pillow. So, on my first morning in the new house, I wake up and immediately notice the damp spot on my cheek. Yep, nothing says "welcome home" like a face full of your own spit.

"Oh, wow," I mumble, sitting up in bed and looking at the room around me. I'd chosen to sleep in the guest room last night. No real reason, only that it was the closest one when I was ready to pass out. The morning view is a good one, as I'm greeted with a view of a maple tree with fire-red leaves that signal autumn is here, and it is breathtaking. I put my feet on the floor and get out of bed, the cold of the hardwood on my soles assisting me in waking up a little faster.

Reaching for a sweatshirt I'd abandoned at the end of the bed before I fell asleep, I'm busy pulling it over my head when I hear what sounds like a car's engine outside of the house. Thrusting my head through the neck hole, making good on my promise to Georgie to stay dressed at all times since prying eyes have binoculars, I hurry over to peer out the window. There's a car idling, which has pulled over inside the lane I share with Austin. I watch as what appears to be a giant chicken trots over to our mailboxes and pulls them both open. The chicken shoves a small bundle inside of each box before it turns and jogs back to its station wagon and pulls away.

Scratching my head, I wonder what I've just witnessed. How often do you see a chicken standing in your lane and putting things in your mailbox? I grab my garden boots and slip them on before making my way down the stairs to trudge out to the mailboxes for my first adventure today.

I open the side door by the kitchen, the closest one to the drive, and as I do, I can see a big red Ford truck slowing down and stopping next to the mailboxes. I can hear the mailbox doors being open and shut, making me think it could be Austin?

As I get closer, I see someone who kind of resembles Austin, or the Austin I remember, sitting behind the steering wheel. I raise my hand and wave, making sure to also smile really wide so he can see it's me. Here I am, standing and waving at this guy like I'm royalty, or a homecoming queen, as his eyes lock with mine. My pulse quickens—I know that face. It's him.

Surely he's going to wave back. Of course he will now that he sees it's me. We'd made each other laugh and we'd gotten along well. So, yes, I fully expect this man to see me and recognize me, and at least...I don't know, nod his head?

So I keep waving.

And he keeps staring.

And...nothing.

He sits there for another awkward second or two before he does us both a favor and pulls away.

"Well," I gripe under my breath as I watch him speed up his driveway, a cloud of dust in his wake, "that's not very welcoming of you, Mr. Porter."

I walk down my driveway to where it meets the shared lane. Spencer had mentioned the realtor telling him this whole area used to be farmland before the owners split off a parcel about ten years ago, intending it for rentals. That's how my two-story house came to be. It was first rented out, then sold to an older, retired woman. When she passed away, the house went on the market, Spencer found it, and voilà—now I've got a home.

When I reach the bank of mailboxes—and by bank, I mean there's two of them—the door to mine is ajar. Peering inside, I find two things. One, the local newspaper. Wagging it in the air, I now know what the guy, or chicken, was dropping off earlier.

The other is a small envelope with nothing on the front of it. Eyeing the note, I hesitate, but then I open it. I'll be honest, I'm half expecting it to maybe be a weird "welcome to the block" note from Austin.

In case you weren't told, your boundary for your home, as in the property line that separates us, is the boxwood hedge in your backyard. Respectfully, I ask that you don't cross it. Thanks.

My jaw goes slack. I read it again, making sure those are the actual words I'm reading with my very own eyes. Is he serious?

"No muffins, Austin?" I call out to no one in particular. "Not very Southern of you, sir. I expected at least a loaf of bread."

Eyeing the hedge, I crumple the note and shove it into the pocket of my pajamas as I make my way back to the kitchen for my first cup of coffee of the morning.

If this is any indication of what life is gonna be like here, I'm gonna need all the caffeine I can get.

THREE

Dex

"So," the man standing behind the counter starts, pushing his glasses up his nose as he squints my way. "You're saying that you want someone to come out to your place and trim back a hedge?"

Only in a small town can you run out to do some errands and slip into a conversation at a hardware store that may help you find a landscaper. Well, fingers crossed.

I nod. "That's exactly it."

He gives me a knowing smile. "I may know someone. Where do you live?"

"On the old Main Road, near the intersection of Highway 50."

"Not a lot of houses out that way." The man's mouth twitches. "Are you on the front of the old Porter farm?"

"The old Porter farm?" What does he mean? "I know it's a Porter who lives there now."

"That's Austin and Levi Porter's grandparents' old farm," the man acknowledges as he finishes ringing me up. "Mr. Porter passed away a few months back and left the place to

Mary, Austin's and Levi's mother. You must be in the house that is at the front. I know it was for sale not long ago."

"Yep, that's me." And only in small towns can you have a chat turn into a who's who in the area, with the local store-keeper informing you of your property's history. This guy is better than Google.

"If it's the hedge I'm thinking of, the one that gives the farmhouse at the back some privacy from your property, then no."

My head tilts to an odd angle on its own. "No?"

"No," he repeats himself, looking at me woefully. "I don't know anyone who will touch that with a ten-foot pole."

Yet things seemed to be going so well. "Why?"

"That boxwood hedge has been around for as long as I can remember. The family must have planted it there years and years ago for it to be as high as it is. I think it was six feet tall the last time I saw it?" he muses, scratching his chin.

"And that is exactly why I need to trim it back." I pull out my wallet to pay for the painting supplies in my cart.

The older gentleman shakes his head. "Ain't no one gonna come and take that job on, I'm sorry to say."

"You're kidding." I'm truly baffled. "Why?"

"That hedge was like the Holy Grail to Mrs. Porter when she was alive. She was the only one who trimmed it back. After she passed, Mr. Porter took it over, but I've got no clue who is taking care of it now. Must be Austin?" He shakes his head again. "That's the other hurdle. Between you and me, we've all seen how unhappy Austin's been since that injury. With the legend of that hedge being so precious––coupled with the fact that the owner of it is now, let's say, tough to deal with––I think finding someone to take care of it may be a mission."

I never thought I'd have to go outside of the local area for something like this.

"So no one will do it?"

"You can try, but I'll be surprised if you can get anyone on board to help." He looks at the cash register. "That's seventy-nine dollars and twenty-four cents, please."

I swipe my credit card and ponder the fact that the one thing standing between me and the view of my dreams is an ancient boxwood hedge that I'll probably never get anyone to help me do anything with.

"Oh, don't listen to him," someone in line behind me says, handing me a business card. "I'm a gardener and would be happy to come by and take a look."

I glance down and see the name on the card. "Thanks, Eric," I say as I slip the card into the back pocket of my jeans. "I'll give you a call very soon."

"Good luck to both of you," the man behind the counter snorts. "As the saying goes, 'May you go with God.'"

I fight the urge to roll my eyes and keep my attention on my new friend, Eric. "Seriously. Thank you."

He smiles, his eyes bouncing to the man, who is still chuckling at his own joke behind the counter, then back to mine. "I'm around, just let me know when you're ready."

I walk out of the Sweetkiss Creek hardware store a little more educated than when I'd gone in. Georgie knew that I was living on the old Porter farm, she had to, and didn't say anything. Why?

Ambling across the small parking lot, I toss my purchases into my car before grabbing my grocery list and jogging over to the store. Time to stock up the fridge.

I'd barely made it down the first aisle when a familiar voice calls my name. When I spin around, I'm not even one bit surprised, although, I am grateful for the serendipity to see Georgie again.

"This is awesome," she says as she gently nudges my grocery cart with hers. "I love that you live here now."

"I guess in a small town, you can't hide much, huh?"

"Nope," she says with a wink as she grabs a package of cookies and tosses them into her cart.

"I'm glad I ran into you, I've got a bone to pick," I say, putting my cart in front of hers so she can't get away quickly. "Why didn't you tell me about Austin living on the farm—that it's his grandparents' home?"

"Oh, man. I know. I should have." Georgie grimaces. "I was afraid you'd find out he was there full time and then see what a jerk he's become and you wouldn't want to move in. We didn't even tell Spencer about his connection—plus, to add salt to the wound, Austin tried to buy your house."

"He did?" My voice hitches with surprise.

She nods her head slowly. "And he wasn't happy when Spencer bought it."

"Headlines, Georgie. These are headlines. Things you lead with. I would have liked to have known what I was getting in my next-door neighbor, you know."

"I know, but look, in the funny way things work out, I was telling Levi about seeing you. He says hi, by the way." She grins, interrupting herself. "I love how interested he is in what I do and have to say."

"Yeah, yeah," I say with sarcastic humor, rolling my eyes playfully. "I get it, you found Prince Charming."

"I did, and it turns out the good prince may have work for you."

If she was trying to pivot and change the subject, she did a good job.

"Really?" I start to move my grocery cart out of her path. "That's awesome."

"The thing is, as he put it, it's got to be the right person to do the job." She turns serious, reaching out and grasping my forearms. "Which I fully believe you are, but it could be a bit of a claustrophobic job, if you take it."

"Claustrophobic. Would I be in a small tunnel or a box?"

She leans on the handle of her grocery cart. "The brothers are partners. Levi does a lot of work, but the deal he made with Austin was that he, Austin, would take care of running the day-to-day business of their rental properties here in Sweetkiss Creek when Levi was out on the road coaching."

It's not often you get a family that has two incredible sports players in its family tree, but to have brothers who both played in the NFL is saying something. Levi retired about a year ago, but only kind of; these days, he travels with his old team, the Carolina Cardinals, and coaches the offensive line. I know from chats with Georgie that he loves doing it, they are based in Charlotte after all, but it still takes him away from home more than he planned, even if he's got more flexibility these days.

"I take it Austin is not holding up his end of the deal when Levi's gone?"

"Nope. And therein lies the rub." Georgie leans against her grocery cart and shakes her head. "Look, I wouldn't be presenting this to you, but the fact that you live right next to him seems to be a sign."

"Yeah. 'No access granted' is what that sign says," I mumble.

Georgie ignores me. "I know from talking to Spencer that you've worked for some real challenging personalities, but you've always been able to handle them well. I think his exact words were that you do it with grace." She flashes a megawatt smile, the kind that probably gets her anything she wants without even trying. "Which made me wonder if Austin can be one more challenge to add to your list?"

"You make me sound like the Pied Piper of personal assistants," I say. "Why haven't you guys hired anyone sooner?"

She shrugs. "We've talked about it, as a family, but it hasn't been until recently that Levi realized how many balls are being dropped. He's home for two days right now, and I'll barely see him because he's out at an apartment organizing new carpet for a new tenant, and then he has a walk-through for someone who's moving out. After that, he's got another appointment, but now we're in the territory where I lose track, so all going well, I'll see him for dinner tonight before he's out the door tomorrow morning for a flight."

I can hear the stress in her voice, never mind the fact she hardly took a breath during her monologue. "That sounds hectic."

"It is." She looks at me. "Is it convenient that you live next door to Austin now? Yes. Am I trying to get you to take this job because it'll help my home life calm down some? Yes, but I swear I wouldn't be asking if I didn't know how awesome you are at what you do."

"Now you're just trying to woo me."

"Is it working?"

"A little."

"Will it help if I tell you that you won't always have to deal with Austin, at least not in person if that's what you prefer? I'm sure we can set up an email check-in system or something that works for both of you."

On one hand, it sounds like it could work. But on the other, it sounds like a lot of, well, work.

"Let me think about it, okay?"

"Okay." She hugs me. "I won't keep you hostage talking about this any longer, but remember if you need anything, just ask."

I start to roll my cart away, but then stop and call out to Georgie as she's about to turn down the aisle.

"Hey, Georgie," I say. "Do you have any idea why a chicken would deliver my mail?"

* * *

Who would have thought that running errands today would give me quite the education? From the history of where I live to a mailman who's also a performer for kids' parties. Who knew?

The whole experience had given me lots to think about on my drive back home. I no sooner pull into the driveway when movement from the back lawn pulls my attention. I stay put behind the wheel of my car, watching the German shepherd as it slinks stealthily toward my back porch and climbs the steps.

The dog is big but also looks skinny, making me wonder whether or not it's been fed recently. My animal lover instincts are kicking in, begging me to rush to its side, but let's be real—this is a strange dog. Like, stranger danger level ten. It's not just any dog, but a German shepherd, the kind they use in police forces to take down bad guys. So, pardon me if I'm not leaping out of my car to give it a warm welcome.

I eye the distance between me and the front door, mentally calculating if I can make it inside without becoming a human chew toy. The song "Galvanize" by the Chemical Brothers begins to play in the background of my mind. The dog is watching me, too, which is only slightly terrifying. Maybe if I time it just right, I can sprint to the house and slam the door before Cujo decides to pounce.

Taking a deep breath, I make my move, flinging the car door open and launching myself out like a sprinter at the Olympics. My heart is pounding, and I'm halfway to the house when I hear the sound of paws thudding behind me. I quicken my pace, pumping my legs faster and praying I don't trip over my own feet.

But of course, I do. Just as I reach the porch steps, I feel something warm and furry against my legs, and the next thing

I know, I'm face-planting into the dirt. My thoughts are racing: *This* is it. *This* is how I die.

But instead of teeth sinking into my skin, I feel...wetness. On my cheek. I crack one eye open to find the dog standing over me, its big brown eyes filled with pure, unadulterated joy as it licks my face like I'm a popsicle on a hot day.

"Okay, okay." Sitting up slowly, laughing, I try to push the exuberant, loving pup away. "I get it. You're not going to eat me." Scratching the dog's neck, I notice there's no collar, which makes my stomach both sink in sadness and also do a dance of happiness. Sad, because I was hoping to reunite this sweetie with its owner, but happy because...well, I like dogs, so if we get to hang out a little longer that's fine by me.

I grab my groceries from the car and head inside, certain as I approach my door that this animal will probably take off or, perhaps, curl up on the porch where she was before. Either way, I'm not expecting it to prance inside in front of me, leading the way in, as I swing the door open.

Laughing, I follow my new friend inside and close the door behind me. "Come on in, why don't ya?"

I'm no stranger to having a pet, and I miss my dog. My dad had a lab that used to also double as my dog, as in I'd steal it when I could so I had a running buddy, but when I moved I promised to leave him so that my dad had company.

I second-guess my judgment for having let this dog in, following him as he wanders room to room, inspecting my things. When we enter the living room, he spots a pile of blankets I'd tossed in a corner in an unpacking flurry earlier today. I watch as the animal turns in a circle, over and over again, landing in a heap in the center of the fabric. Within a matter of seconds, a soft snore rises from its body and its eyes are closed tight.

Shaking my head, I make my way back to the kitchen to put my groceries away. I start digging around for something I can use as water and food bowls for the animal. I'm not a horrible hostess; I want to make sure my four legged visitor gets taken care of if he, or she, needs room service.

A few hours later, after I've grilled a couple of steaks for us —filet mignon because why not?—I glance out the window and see it's getting dark. My plan had been to hop in the car and drive to a few neighboring houses—no, not Austin's... friendly neighbors—and ask about the dog. With night falling I realize I need to go now.

Swiping my keys, I shake them in the air and call out to the strange animal. "Come on, sweetie. Let's go find your family."

When I approach his makeshift bed, I notice the dog is shaking. Trembling excessively is probably the better way to describe it. Kneeling down, I put my hand on its back and pet its fur slowly. "What's going on, buddy?"

No sooner are the words out of my mouth than a loud crack sounds in the air around us followed closely by a clap of thunder. There's a pitter-patter of raindrops drumming repetitively on the roof as a thunderstorm rolls in around us.

"Fine. You win, we'll wait til morning." I can't prove it, but I swear that dog stopped shaking as soon as I acquiesced.

Yawning, sleep begins to overtake me, leading me to make my way upstairs to head to bed. I do my nightly routine, washing my face and doing the girl things I like to do, and when I walk into my bedroom, I find my unexpected guest on the floor, next to my side of the bed, already asleep.

"Goodnight, stinker," I whisper as I climb over my new friend and turn out the light. As I get settled under the covers, I glance outside my window, realizing for the first time that I have a full view from here across the field to Austin's house.

It looks lonely over there. It looks cold and dark, like a haunted house that you'd see in a cartoon. There's one lone light that burns bright in an upstairs window, and as I watch, it's suddenly extinguished. It's as if someone was there and knew I was watching.

The dog's snoring gets louder beside me as I lay my head on my pillow. The vision of Austin's light dampening on replay in my head as the sound of raindrops falling overhead lulls me to sleep.

FOUR

Austin

Driving back to Sweetkiss Creek from the family farm today, I had to tip my hat to my mother: she had gotten me out of the house for breakfast this morning. Only she could trick me into coming out to see her so she can check on me. If I asked her outright if that was her plan, no doubt she'd deny it. That's fine. In retrospect, I know her well enough that I should have caught on to what she was doing.

Her ask? If I could help move a few pieces of furniture that she'd sold to the porch. Only when I arrived—surprise!— she didn't need my help any longer. Like magic, the people she was expecting had already stopped by and picked up the items. So, of course she invites me to stay for breakfast instead.

The drive back had taken me a little longer than the drive there. I'd had one of those weird moments like I wasn't sure I knew where I was. It was disorienting, to say the least, but made me slow down and err on this side of caution.

It had started with the potholes in the road. I don't remember them being this bumpy. I know these roads like the back of my hand, so I'm curious why today they feel harder to navigate. As if when I look at the road ahead, I don't know what is coming around the next turn, even though it's a familiar stretch of road that I grew up on. Kind of like my life right now, isn't it? No wonder my own mother has taken to trickery to get me over to visit.

Coming over a small rise, I can see my property ahead, alerting me that I'm home. Slowly, I let my gaze slide over to my new neighbor's home. There's a bright yellow van parked in her driveway, making me wonder what's already broken down that she needs to have fixed.

That house was, at one time, part of my grandparents' property. They'd built it as a rental, but it had come in handy when they needed money to help because crops weren't their best one year. The house was there for them to sell off so they could put the cash into savings.

The nostalgic part of me always thought I'd be in a position to get it back one day. Truly. I'd thought when I hit it big that I would be the one: the member of the family who could swoop in and save my people. Not that anyone needs saving, but you know, I wanted to be the caretaker for once. The son who when their mom says, "I need to pay a bill," he's the one who pays it.

Slowing down, I put on my blinker to turn into the lane, keeping my focus on my end game of getting home. However, it only takes one word on the side of that van to draw my attention and set off an alarm.

Landscaping.

Slamming my foot on the brake, I throw my truck into reverse, backing up at a ridiculous rate of speed so I can pull into Bex's driveway. I'm going so fast, my truck all but slides to a stop behind the van. I hop out, and when I look across the back lawn, I find Bex standing near the hedge that separates our properties with a large workman beside her.

"Hey!" I call out, marching to where they stand huddled together. "Are you looking at that hedge?"

I swear I see her bristle from here. As Bex stands up taller as I approach, I realize I haven't seen her—like *seen* her—since before my injury. I'd forgotten how utterly drop-dead beautiful she is. Her face breaks into a huge smile when she sees me, taking me off guard.

There's a stab at a distant memory, reminding me that at one time, I thought she was really cute. Like, I wanted to kiss her cute...not that it matters now.

No one wants a defect like me.

"Hey, Austin," she calls out. She turns and says something to the man before she jogs over to me. "It's really nice to see you. Crazy we're neighbors, huh?"

"Yeah, it's nuts." I point to the hedge. "Are you thinking of doing something to that?"

"Well, yes," she says, parking her hands on her hips. "I'm having it trimmed back."

"Trimming it." Threading my arms across my chest, I pull myself tight in the center as I narrow my eyes and stare at her. "You need to ask my permission, Bex. It's on my property."

"Actually, Austin," Bex says, shaking her head as she pulls out a piece of paper from a folder she's holding and hands it to me, "I'm the kind of person who does my due diligence. I checked the country records this morning so I could find out where the property lines are." She flips to a page with a sketch of our section on it, pointing to a red line. "That line there, the one that's on the other side of the hedge, is an indication of where my property boundary is."

Holding the paper in my hands, I begin to feel uncharacteristically full of rage. My hands begin shaking and, out of the corner of my eye, I notice Bex taking a step away from me.

"This," I say, holding the paper in the air, "is from your realtor?"

She nods. "I'm happy to put you in touch with Kaci, but she's on vacation visiting her best friend."

"I know who Kaci is." She's the local realtor I tried to talk into selling me this house out from under Spencer, but she wouldn't do it. That's a smart woman right there.

"Sorry, Austin," Bex says. "I was going to come over to see you about this once the landscaper left."

"Well, this is the first I've heard about this hedge being an issue. This land has been in my family for a long time, and I know this hedge was put in by my grandparents."

"I get it." Bex nods, her face morphing as she takes on an expression like she's dealing with a toddler. "I want to find a compromise if we can."

"Okay." I drop my arms to my sides. "Will you consider not trimming the hedge in some way?"

She sighs, flipping her hair over her shoulder and treating me to a whiff of some kind of citrus fruit. I do love oranges. "I really want the view, Austin. I want to be able to sit in my backyard and see the pretty pond that's between our homes."

I can't help it. I roll my eyes. "Then take a picture."

"Not the kind of answer I was hoping for."

"Well, you're not the kind of neighbor I was hoping for." Not at all. I like my neighbors to be less attractive and to at least smell bad. But this one? She's like sunshine and sugar kisses, and if she flips her hair one more time...

"Wow. This is not a productive conversation." She snorts and points to my truck. "I think you should leave."

Grunting my agreement, I take a step and my foot lands in a puddle, remnants of the storm the night before. Letting out a burdened sigh, I look down to see my new Converse covered in mud. When I look back up, Bex stands before me with her lips twitching.

"Go ahead. We'll see who has the last laugh," I say flippantly over my shoulder as I head back to the truck.

"You know, I don't need you to stop by here and be so rude to me, Austin." Her voice sounds like she's close. When I

31

look back over my shoulder, I see she's following me, wagging a finger in the air.

Here we go.

"Oh?" As I get to the truck, I open the door and pause, putting her in my sights. "What do you need me to do?"

"Nothing. I need nothing from you. I just wanted to get along with the person I live closest to."

"Well, if you want to get along, it's easy. Do. Not. Touch. That. Hedge."

Bex shakes her head. "I can see you're not wanting to discuss this right now, so we'll table it."

I let my eyes roll to the heavens, again, and I say a quick prayer. Slamming the truck door shut again, I spin around faster than a kitchen blender. "We're not tabling anything. Not now, not tomorrow, not next week. We're going to call this a done deal; no one will be touching that hedge anytime soon, not without my permission first."

"Austin," Bex growls, putting her fingers to her temples. "That's the thing. I don't need your permission. I can do what I want to do to that hedge by the word of law." She waves her folder in the air. "If I want to, I could plow those hedges..."

The mere suggestion makes me see red. It's time to go. My lips tighten into a straight line and I feel my pulse quicken as I turn on my heel, fling the truck's door open and hop in. I slam the door shut and finally find peace in the silence of the cab.

Once I turn over the ignition, I roll down the window and point a finger directly at Bex. "Do not do anything to that hedge. Got it? Nothing. No. Thing. Not a thing. Ever."

"Austin," Bex starts to say, but again, I'm seeing red. The smart part of me knows that she isn't to blame for where this anger is coming from, but my irrational part? He's on fire at the moment and ready to burn everything down. And I do mean everything.

I need to get him home and lock this Austin in a room.

"Nope." I throw the gears into reverse and start to pull out of her driveaway. I make sure I can see where she's standing and confirm she's nowhere near the truck. For effect, of course, I hit the gas. Hard. Maybe a little too hard, in retrospect, because I also *may* have sped up a touch as I was backing up.

So, no, I don't see that puddle my tire lands in, spraying mud all over Bex in the process. But you can bet I hear about it.

Her high-pitched scream stops me in my tracks. I hit the brakes, only when I do, the truck is already rolling into another puddle and the friction of my stopping causes another wave to rise up and splash out, covering the parts of her that aren't already under mud a nice thick coat of murky browny-gray.

I'm horrified. Even after being as mad as I was a second ago, I surely did not mean for this to escalate so quickly.

I go to open the door, but Bex holds up her hand.

"Go." She points one long, mud-covered arm toward my house. "Just go home and leave me alone."

"But…"

She shakes her head, looking at me with what appears to be confusion in her eyes. "What happened to you?"

* * *

"You did what?"

Sighing, I lay on Emma's sturdy travel massage table and repeat myself. "I accidentally sprayed her with mud." Five tiny digits dig into the flesh around my shoulder. My karma, obviously, for my earlier actions. "Ouch."

"Sorry." Emma snickers. "I must be channeling your new neighbor's irritation and it's coming through. How can you spray someone with mud by accident?"

The sound of someone clearing their throat echoes in the small space. Since Emma's here with me, I quickly deduce it's Amy, my housekeeper. She'd shown up today with a homemade tuna casserole, and two days early for her usual cleaning day, but that's a conversation for another day.

"Excuse me, Austin?" she all but purrs. "Your sheets in the bedroom have been changed and all of the laundry is put away. Need anything else before I go?"

"Nope, thank you, Amy." I keep my face pressed into the hole cut into the table. Look, I know she likes me, but I try to watch everything I do so I don't lead her on, you know? She seems nice enough except for the time I caught her changing in my bedroom.

"Okay," she says slowly. I can hear her footsteps as she makes her way toward the foyer. "See you soon."

As she leaves, Emma's fingers dig in even more. It feels like she's trying to rip my muscles apart.

"For someone who's supposed to be here aiding me with my recovery, you're doing a terrible job."

There's a pause as her fingers are replaced with what must be the pointy tip of her elbow. She leans into me with all of her weight, grunting in the process while I bite my tongue so I don't emit the high-pitched squeal that's currently caught in my throat.

"Terrible?" She eases off only to come back with more force. It's like a sumo wrestler has taken over the body of my physical therapist. "I'd watch it if I was you. Although, saying that, I need to make sure I'm nowhere near you the next time we're in the driveway."

"It was an accident," I whine as she taps me on the head lightly, her signal that it's time for me to roll over.

"Austin, you need to deal with your boundaries here. First up, that maid."

Sighing, I throw my hands in the air. "She has a crush."

"On her boss. Didn't you tell me you found some socks and that some of your T-shirts were missing after she started?"

"Well, yes," I confess. "Underwear, too, but I could have lost them myself."

"And you hired her to be here once a week, and now she shows up at least twice a week?"

"She said she was worried and wanted to make sure the house was clean."

"Austin." I can hear the shock in her tone. "No one does that. Get a new maid. And go tell your neighbor you're sorry." Greased hands begin massaging the bottoms of my feet, sending me straight to heaven. Emma knows my soft spot. "But, really, I know another cleaning service and I'm happy to send you their details. Discreet and old."

"Old?"

She cackles. "Little old retired women work for the company, and I think for you, it's perfect."

I'm seriously contemplating Emma's suggestion when the door that enters into my kitchen opens and closes, the screen door slamming with such force I think momentarily it came off its hinges.

"Austin!" My mother's voice echoes through the house. For someone who was so happy to see me earlier today, she doesn't sound so pleased now.

"In here," I call out, lifting my head up and squinting as she appears in the room and beside me within seconds. "Good thing I'm not meditating or doing something important, you know. Like working with my physical therapist."

"Hi, Emma Rose," Mom says, acknowledging the thera-pist––with her first and last name oddly enough––who has worked with both of her sons over the years, helping us through various injuries. But make no mistake, her focus is on me. "You know, Austin, I'd love to know why your sweet new neighbor who we just spoke to is outside of her house, standing under a hose cleaning mud off herself and wishing all the evils of the underworld on you and your kin?"

"Yeah," Levi agrees, waltzing into the room behind her. "Since we're your kin, we need to know why we're being cursed." He sees I have company and waves. "Hey, Emma."

Emma's hands stop moving. I open one eye only to find her looking at me and shaking her head. "I'm gonna give y'all a few minutes to talk this over. Holler when you're ready."

I push myself so I'm sitting upright when Mom parks herself in front of me wearing her sternest expression. "I'm serious, Austin Leonardo Porter. What has that girl done to you?"

I wince hearing the use of my middle name. This means she's really mad, and it also means that Levi is due to start laughing.

"Leonardo," Levi begins on cue. "Like a Teenage Mutant Ninja Turtle."

"Shush," Mom says, not even looking at him. She points one long finger my way. "I want to know why you were in such a mood today that you verbally assaulted your new neighbor and then covered her in mud?"

"Like a pig." Levi is still smirking. I can see his mug over my mother's shoulder, but she won't turn around. So she has no idea what I'm dealing with—sibling superiority of the worst kind. "Maybe we should have called you 'Peppa' or 'Porky' and not Leonardo."

"Maybe you should..." I start to tell him off, but the moment I flex my hand and try to get off the table, Mom places her hand on my shoulder and firmly puts me back into place.

"Don't you dare move. I've had it."

"You think you've had it? What about me?" I toss my hands in the air. "I'm the one who is sitting here alone recovering every day. By myself."

She sniffs. "That was your decision. Not ours. Don't take that out on us."

"I can do what I want, I'm the one who has to start over." Even I'm cringing as the sound of my whiny voice fills the room.

"You can, but when you do, your actions affect us. And don't forget I'm your mother. I brought you into this world, I can take you out of it."

She's used that one on me before. "I'm an adult now."

"Prove it."

"It's not like I invited you guys to come by here—"

This is when Levi gives me the impression he's also had enough. "That's it," he interjects, clapping his hands together. Finally someone comes to my defense for once. But my, how the tables turn. Where there should've been brotherly love, he's taking a different side. "You need to quit talking to our mother like she's not worth your time. In fact, you need to stop talking to all of us like we're an imposition. I think we're all tired of it, Austin."

"Et tu, Brute?" Slowly, I lower myself back onto the massage table and begin rubbing my temples. Even though it feels good to spout off some steam, it also doesn't. It's hollow anger, which is kind of how I feel most of the time.

"Don't quote words at me," Levi huffs. "I don't want to hear you talking to our mother like that, nor do I want you talking to me the way you have been. I can put up with a lot, but it's been too much and going on for too long."

"Really? You're not the one who was forced into early retirement. You chose to leave."

I thought that would shut him up. It only adds fuel to his fire.

"You have a torn Achilles. You could heal and get back on the field, but you have to want it bad enough. One thing I don't see from you is that kind of want." Levi throws his hands in the air. "I've watched you treat our mother like crap, witnessed your meltdowns for months now, and not said a thing, only now they're spilling onto your neighbor. How long until you start treating Georgie poorly? Or even Emma for that matter?"

I'm offended. "You really think I'd lash out at either one of them—"

"Yes," he interjects. "I do. Have you seen yourself lately and paid attention to how you act? You are a train wreck, man."

"Stop that," I say, wagging a finger of warning his way.

"Or what?" he taunts. "You gonna come after me? Yell at me? Splash me with mud?" Levi snorts sarcastically. "Of course you won't. You're too busy avoiding me and your responsibilities to our business. We agreed that when I'm on the road, you are supposed to be the point person for our properties. Remember that?"

"Stop it, Levi." My tone is clipped and quick, but I need him to get it. He's pushing too hard.

Mom, who had been standing with her hands clasped and her head swiveling from side to side like she's watching a tennis match, pipes up. "I'm not going to stop him, Austin, because your brother has a point. It's aggressive, but it's true."

At least she gets my subtle hint.

"I'm being aggressive because he is," Levi grumbles, sounding a lot like he did when we were teens.

"I'm not being aggressive, you are." Okay. Pot meet kettle.

"Boys." Mom comes over to the table and motions for me to scoot over. Once I do, she hops up beside me and throws an arm around me. "I think this is a tough love moment for you, but it had to happen, Austin. We can't go on like this, *you* can't go on like this."

When I look into her eyes, I see her hurt. Her pain. And

it's not only hers, it's the pain and hurt she has for me. For a son who isn't able to be there for her like he used to be.

And I hate it. I need to do better.

"I'm sorry," I whisper, dragging my eyes to hers. I can't look at Levi. I'm not ready to deal with him yet. I want to fix things with our mom first. "I don't know why I'm compelled to be such a grump."

At that moment, something outside my window in the distance catches my eye. Turning my head to see what it is, I spy a lone German shepherd crouched in my yard, and if I'm not mistaken, it's actually eyeballing me. I swear. That dog is looking me square in the eyes as he does a number two. Then, with two swift kicks of his back feet as if he was covering it, he takes off and races across the field to Bex's house.

"Are. You. KIDDING ME?" I scream, jumping off the table and barely managing to wrap the sheet around me that covers my nether regions. Throwing open the front door, I get a little jump scare when I almost trip over Emma sitting on my front steps holding a book.

"Why are you screaming?" she asks.

"Because I want some quiet, but my house is like Grand Central Station today and that dog just dropped a turd in my yard," I say, spit flying from my mouth. Wow. I do *not* recognize myself anymore.

"Say it, don't spray it," Emma mutters, wiping off her book. "You know, your family has a point. You have been totally on edge the last few months and you're getting..."

"I know. Worse. I'm worse and I'm horrible and aggressive."

"I was going to say you seem really down and depressed and like you need to talk to someone." She shrugs, then turns her back to me, sticking her nose back into her book. "But hey, what do I know? I'm just a physical therapist trying to read a book on the porch of the grumpiest dude in Sweetkiss Creek."

A sound at the door behind me pulls my attention. Spinning around, I find my mother and Levi standing in its frame, both with arms crossed.

"You're out of control," Levi says in the calmest voice I've heard in months.

"Out of control?" I repeat, trying to keep my eyes from bugging out of their sockets as I jab a finger in the direction of where the dog was squatting, then swing it toward Bex's house. "Didn't you see that dog? How would she like it if I came over to her yard and took a dump?"

"Oh, Austin," Levi groans, rubbing his forehead like he's suddenly got a migraine.

"I know. She wouldn't," I mutter, but the words sound hollow even to me.

"Don't act like I'm on your side, 'cause I'm not," Levi clarifies, and I can't tell if it's more for my benefit or his. Not that it matters. Nothing does these days.

"Fine. Totally okay by me." But even as the words leave my mouth, I feel a flicker of doubt. Maybe Levi's right. Maybe I am losing it. But, please. Like I'm going to admit that.

Mom flips her hair over her shoulder and rolls her eyes, the ultimate gesture of motherly disappointment. "I should never have let you move out."

Her words hit harder than they should. I'm suddenly aware of how quiet the room has gotten, the tension hanging in the air like a thick fog. I want to snap back, to remind them both that I'm still me, but I don't have it in me.

I know I'm on a rocky path, that I'm out of control and have been. Truth is, I've gotten so used to feeling bad that I'm not sure I know how to feel good or like there's anything to look forward to anymore. I don't know when it happened nor how, I just know it has. And it sucks.

Instead, I stare at the door, thinking about Bex and that infuriating dog. Thinking about how everything is spiraling out of control, and how I've never felt so lost. But mostly, I'm thinking about everyone else's expectations. I grit my teeth, feeling the weight pressing down on me like a stubborn fog.

"Don't worry about me," I say, forcing a smirk that feels more like a grimace. "I'm just getting started."

But even as the words hang in the air, I know they're a lie.

As my brilliant declaration hangs in the air, I know it's as believable as a cat claiming it's "just looking" at the goldfish. The real question now is: How on earth am I going to untangle this ridiculous mess I've made without turning the world around me into a full-blown soap opera?

FIVE

Dex

I love fall. I love the crunch of leaves under my feet, the feel of the air, and the appearance of warm colors like burnt orange and rust in my wardrobe. It's the best time of year. It's not so cold that I need to bundle up, but there is enough chill to the air that a little heat feels good. Cozy sweaters are worn in abundance, fluffy blankets are pulled out of closets and brought out for a season or two, and smells like pumpkin spice and chai fill the air. At least at my house they do.

From my perch on the sofa, I stare at the fireplace in the corner and make a silent agreement with myself to light it this week if the weather stays like this.

I'd woken up this morning in a state of panic with heart palpitations banging their way through my chest and leg cramps so intense I'd had to slam my foot against the wall and press it firmly and with so much force that it felt like I was trying to put my leg through it. It's the only way I can get relief when the cramps take control.

Things about Graves' disease I wasn't prepared for: all of it.

Sighing, I close my eyes and rest my head against the back

of the couch. I could have stayed in bed for another few hours, but I've got too much to do. Graves is funny. It robs and depletes you of your energy, but you need to keep going. It's also been robbing me of my hair lately, a shock I had last night when I was in the shower. I don't notice it often, but every now and then when I seem to slip out of what my doctors have noted as remission, I'll suddenly get the symptoms again. When it happens, I just go back to what I know. Taking some pills and working really hard to keep the stress out of my daily routine.

I swipe my prescription bottle from its place on the coffee table and pop one in my mouth. I don't even need water, I'm so used to this now.

I make a beeline for the thermostat on the wall, turning the heater on. As I swallow my pill, my eye is drawn to the yard, which is my next stop. The grass needs to be mowed and I should do some weeding today, but something in the field pulls my gaze toward Austin's house. I'm immediately reminded of who he is now and what I'm dealing with, the hitch in my stomach making me irritated with him for his actions the other day all over again.

"And to think I was going to take that job," I mutter as I grab my gardening gloves and head out into the backyard to get some work done. I'm glad that I told Georgie I needed to think about it. I can't fathom working with that man.

Once I'm outside, I pop my earbuds in and make sure I've got a good playlist pulled up. The first song is Djo's "End of Beginning," my latest favorite tune for those melancholy moments when my internal drama takes center stage.

I get busy with the weeding I have to do, but I can't help glaring across the field at Austin's. Former pro football player who has taken to hiding away in his house like an angry troll. But of course, as soon as I think about this, I remind myself what he's been through—that it can't be easy, especially seeing how it's football season and the NFL is being promoted everywhere you look.

Then there's the issue of the hedge. My hedge. I know I should probably let this one go, but it's hard when I know I'm in the right. I can see myself sitting here, in the backyard, looking out over the pond and to the view of the rolling fields beyond. Future Bex likes this for me.

When I walk over to the hedge to give it a closer inspection, something in the recess of my mind reminds me that boxwood is resilient and can be shaped into anything. If so, I'll show Austin. I'll cut a hole in the middle of this sucker and make a window. Then my shiny butt will be framed when I moon him.

"Bet you'd like to see that with your binoculars, wouldn't you, Mr. Silence of the Lambs?" I growl to myself.

I'm still muttering obscenities when something snuffling my feet makes me jump in the air. When I gain composure, I look down to find one really cute German shepherd staring back up at me.

"You're back, huh?" I lean down and scratch her between the ears. A jangle-ing sound pulls my attention. "You've got a collar on today."

Good. Maybe I can do at least one good deed and get this dog back to its owner, or at least keep it from coming here so much. Whipping my phone out of my back pocket, I pause my playlist before tapping the numbers into my phone.

It rings a few times before sending me to voicemail. Keeping my eye on the dog, whose name is Harley according to the tag, I leave a message with my contact details.

"Here's hoping," I say to no one in particular as I hang up. As I do, I watch Harley slowly lower herself to her belly, staring across the field directly at Austin's.

I follow her gaze; if you ignore the hedge that's practically screaming, "You're not welcome here," it's actually kind of picturesque. Through the leafy barricade, I catch a glimpse of the pond, which is quite charming—if you're into that whole "rustic serenity" thing. It's not exactly the Grand Canal, but it's doing a decent job of looking serene, with its occasional ripple and a few ducks that probably have grander ambitions.

Austin's house is framed by this pastoral scene like it's trying to be the poster child for *Country Living*. I suppose if you squint and ignore the fact that the hedge is having a personal vendetta against my right to a clear view, it's actually quite lovely. It's the kind of scene that makes you want to grab a blanket, a cup of tea, and contemplate life's mysteries—or at least try to figure out how I ended up with such an entertaining neighbor. Oh, the absurdity of it all.

A chill snakes its way down my spine, a gentle reminder that it's fall and tonight could be a cold one. I'm blissfully unaware of the weather patterns here, being from Southern California. I guess to me everywhere is cold until I get used to it.

I make my way back in, Harley hot on my heels. Opening the door to the kitchen, I'm shocked when I'm hit by a wall of frigid air rolling out to greet me.

"What is happening? That's cold!" I exclaim as I sprint over to the thermostat. I thought I'd hit the wrong button, choosing the air-conditioning option and not heat, but no. It's set on heat. The thermostat says it's seventy-eight degrees.

"Liar." I turn the dial up and put my hand to one of the vents in the living room. Yep. Freezing cold air.

Acting fast, because I know I need to fix this now, I pull out my phone again and do a quick search online to find a local heating specialist I can hopefully coerce into coming out today.

* * *

The workman before me looks like he's seen more sunrises than I can count. His face is etched with deep lines, like a comfy and worn leather sofa, each one a testament to years of hard labor or time spent in the sun. His hands are rough, calloused, and marked with scars, evidence of a lifetime spent building, fixing, and toiling. A few strands of silver are threaded through his thick, dark hair, and his eyes still hold a sharp, assessing glint.

"Yep, exactly as I thought," he says as he scribbles on a notepad. "The unit is going to need to be replaced."

"Noooo," I moan. The lurch in my stomach almost pulls me to my knees. "Replaced?"

"That thing is old," he continues, nodding sympathetically. "It's practically a fossil. I'm surprised it's still running at all."

"Great," I say, trying to mask my panic with sarcasm. "So, what's the damage? Do I need to start selling off family heirlooms, or should I just empty my savings account now?"

The repairman chuckles. "Well, it's not quite that bad. But you're definitely looking at a decent chunk of change to get a new unit."

"Perfect. Just what I needed," I mutter. "Another thing to add to my ever-growing list of 'Things I'd Rather Not Deal With Today.'"

He gives me a sympathetic smile. "I know it's a hassle. But a new unit will be more efficient and save you money in the long run."

"Yeah, assuming I don't have to live on ramen noodles to pay for it," I reply, shaking my head. "Well, I guess I'll be shopping for an HVAC unit instead of groceries this week."

"Let me know if you need any recommendations," he says, gathering his tools. "I promise it'll be worth it."

I should sit and let this sink in, but hearing you need to replace a whole heating and cooling unit in your home right before winter does not sound appealing. Nor does it sound inexpensive.

"Out of curiosity, do you know how much they cost?"

He shrugs. "Last one I worked on ran close to eight."

"Eight?" Fingers crossed, I smile his way. "Like eight hundred?"

"That's a stretch," he says. "I wish. More like eight thousand."

I feel ill. It's not like I can call my landlord to come fix this. I *am* the landlord.

He gives me a number to call when I'm ready to order the unit, and I thank him as he walks out to his van to go. Leaving me staring into the distance wondering where I'm going to get that kind of money from right now.

I can't ask Spencer, even though he and Amelia would loan it to me in a heartbeat. Grabbing my phone, I tap on the app for my bank and stare at my balance. This would make the largest dent in what I have managed to save over the years. A scary thought when you have no income coming in.

The realization hits me that I am going to have to work. Seeing as I need a new heating system, I can't take the time now to worry about who it is I'm working for. I need a job and I need it fast.

Sighing, I text Georgie.

> Let Levi know I'm going to call him in the morning about that job. I can start ASAP.

In a matter of seconds, she answers.

> WOO HOO! He'll call tomorrow. Thank you!

Leaning my head against the window, I stare out into the yard, willing this issue to go away. I let my eyes wander over to the front garden beds, which need to be cleaned up a little more, then over to the magnolia trees that line one side of the drive, right where I'd left my car. While I stare at it, something waves in the air, like an errant piece of paper flapping in the wind but seemingly stuck to my windshield.

Curious as to what it is, I head outside, snatching the small piece of paper from its spot behind my windshield wiper and read it. A surge of rage-like heat fills my body as I let the dumb words written on this stupid piece of paper sink in.

If your dog ever, EVER poops on my property again, I will scoop it into a shovel and bring it to your front porch for you to deal with.

To think I ever thought this man was hot. Not just hot, but hot. The kind of hot a man can be when his insides match the outside. But this is the sign that the guy I thought he was isn't there anymore.

I'm stunned. The way he's acted since I arrived is unstable. Irritating. Ridiculous. First, the welcome note. Then, his unhinged incident with the spraying of the mud. Now this?

Fine. You wanna play, football boy, we can play.

I look around the yard, searching for something. Anything. I can't stop the tiny devilish sneer that pulls my lips upwards at the corner when my line of vision lands on one of Harley's little stinky treasures over by a magnolia. Bingo.

I quickly head inside and grab a small baggie and a paper bag. On my way out, I spy some ribbon sticking out of a bag from my present wrapping station (still need to unpack that), and grab a piece. It's Christmas ribbon too, so even more perfect.

Once I have his present prepped, I stomp across the field to Austin's, toss the present onto his porch with a note attached to it of my own, and knock on his door. Within seconds, old man crank bottom opens it, eating a giant red apple, wearing an old football jersey, and glares at me.

I point to the gift. "There. Wrapped up for you in a spectacular package. Is this better? Is that how you want your feces?"

"Do you think I was worried about the presentation?" he says between bites as he steps out onto the porch. "It's the gift that keeps on giving that I worry about."

Do my eyes get pulled to his lips, watching the way they glide across the skin of that piece of fruit as he wraps them around it and takes each big, delicious bite? I could smack myself; since when do someone's lips become this seductive while they're eating? I start to contemplate this when the movement of his jaw as he chews each bite so mindfully drags my attention there. When the chewing stops, my eyes flick to his, only to find him staring at me. Yep. Caught in the act.

I shift my gaze away as he snickers. Ugh. What is my problem? This is a man with an apple. A good-looking man holding an apple. A good-looking man with a sexy jawline who appears to be enjoying eating this apple in front of me.

I need to get a grip.

"I don't really care that it bothers you, Johnny Appleseed. This"—I hold the note he left me in the air—"is insane." I tap the side of my head with my pointer finger. "You're making me crazy and I just moved in."

"That's got to be a record," he says as he takes a lazy bite out of the apple.

"Or a statute of limitations," I zing back.

I don't know what comes over me, but it's like I am sitting in silent witness as my hand lifts itself into the air and all of my fingers clench into a fist except one. I'm not proud, but yes, I hold up my middle finger and flip this man the bird like an unrelenting explorer who has discovered a new mountain range and is lifting their fist in the air. I also do it with such dramatic force that it feels like I may have tweaked my wrist.

"You're such a lady. Perfect addition to the South," he purrs.

I'm so mad I'm spitting tacks. "You're insane. I do not know how anyone on this earth can deal with you."

"Well, good thing you don't really have to," are the last words I hear as the door slams in my face.

With a sickness floating in my tummy, a lightbulb suddenly turns on over my head in true cartoon-realization style.

I have to work with him now.

SIX

Austin

Having my morning coffee on the porch has always been a joy for me, even when times are rough. In fact, I find this morning ritual to be most effective when the going gets tough.

It's not just the way the early light spills over the paddocks, turning the dew on the grass into a soft, glistening haze. It's peaceful out here, just me, my mug, and the view that stretches out across the land. I rent out paddocks to local farmers—cattle now, horses later, and goats coming soon. It's the best part of this place. I get to sit on my porch and watch the slow rhythm of life unfolding before me.

Even the pond—especially that pond—right there in the distance, the one Bex mentioned wanting to see. Too bad that boxwood hedge blocks her view.

I hear my thoughts and I hang my head. Sipping my coffee, I realize I've hit a new low. I should make her feel welcome, but here I am, hiding behind hedges and memories. Seeing the ghost of a crush from my past is obviously spinning me out.

I remember Bex from when she first came to Sweetkiss.

Her hazel eyes were a bright emerald green that day—vivid, alive, like the first breath of spring. Of course, I've thought about her. More than I should, honestly.

The sound of my phone ringing beside me breaks the quiet. The familiar ringtone, *Thunderstruck,* blares out. I don't have to look to know it's my brother.

"What have you done to your neighbor now?" He all but spits the words at me.

I blink, surprised. Bex and I only had our last big row less than twenty-four hours ago. Unless she put it out on social media, I have no clue how he'd know this.

"Why? Has she called the police on me?"

"No. I hadn't had the chance to tell you, but I hired someone to help us out. Well, to help me out, and it's Bex. She's already tried to quit before she even started, citing irreconcilable differences."

I can't help but chuckle. Of course this is my life.

"Don't laugh, Austin. It's not funny. You need to make nice, and fast, or I'm going to kill you. Until you sort your issues out, she'll go through Georgie or myself, which is not ideal since we're both busy. So, I need you to stop being such a child."

"Why do I need to be on my best behavior for her or for anyone?"

"Didn't we just go over this with Mom? You have got to get a grip. Seriously, shut up and get over it."

Oof. I really don't like it when someone tells me to get over it.

"I don't need to—"

But Levi is ready and cuts me off. "Come on, Austin. Stop it. At one time, you got along with her. You got along with everyone."

How do I explain that, yes I did. I got along with all kinds of people, and I definitely got along with Bex. I thought about her a lot, and now here she is and I'm broken.

"Well, things changed, didn't they?"

"Look, I need you to work with her, okay? I need you two to get along so I can be on the road with the team, and in Charlotte when I need to be, and so Georgie isn't stressed. We're in a position where we can have help, so we do. Please, work with her. For me."

"But we want to kill each other. I think she would gladly put a pillow over my head and watch the life leave my body as she smothered me to death."

"Well, you both need to push past it together, then. I need you to play nice. As far as I'm concerned, this is a you thing."

"She's fifty percent of the issue, too," I say, aware I'm quite maturely (insert maniacal laugh here) laying blame when it's not needed. I know in my heart of hearts she doesn't deserve this, but it feels good to have someone to be irritated with right now. Granted my irritation is blind, irrational, and uncalled for, so we'll call it a slow leak for my pent-up anger.

"Look, no matter what you say, it's done. Bex is working for us. We've had a carpeting issue in one of the rental properties and need someone to keep an eye on the painters as they get an apartment ready to rent out. Can I count on you?"

I lean back in my chair, staring out at the cattle moving slowly in the paddock. My attitude has kept people away from me, which is how I like it. How I needed it. But now?

"Yeah," I finally say, the word heavy in my mouth. "I can do it."

"Good," Levi replies, his tone softening just a fraction. "And, Austin, maybe give her a chance, huh? She's not the enemy."

Therein lies my issue. I let out a breath, watching the steam rise from my coffee. "Yeah, I'll try."

"See that you do," Levi says, and then the line goes dead.

I sit there for a moment, the phone still in my hand, the quiet returning to the morning. I've always been good at keeping people at a distance, but now, with Bex back in my life, I'm starting to wonder if that's the right move anymore. Maybe it's time to stop running from the past and start figuring out what the hell I want for my future.

SEVEN

$\mathcal{D}$ex

I 'd woken up this morning with a sore wrist (lesson learned from flipping the bird, I guess) and to a bevy of emails forwarded my way from Levi. He'd messaged me last night and warned me that there was a lot to sift through, but twenty-three emails for my first morning, and over my first cup of coffee, already has me rethinking my salary negotiations.

The Porter boys have a lot of properties they own, and now rent out, around town. From the list Levi gave me, it appears I'll be handling at least four apartment buildings. They have more, but they hired on-site managers for those, and they also own a few industrial warehouse spaces, too, but those are handled by a separate commercial management group.

Today's mission is to go out to one of the units with two large apartments. It's in town and used to be an old Victorian home that's been redone with an apartment on each floor. Levi asked me to introduce myself to the tenants and also to take pictures of the damage done to the carpet in Mrs. Rosenblatt's. She lives on the first floor, likes to collect glass animals and cross-stitched pillows, and apparently manages to clog her shower drain at least once a month.

"So, the last time this happened, you didn't notice it was clogged?" Looking at the floor beside her tub, there's a giant dark stain. It also smells a little like sangria in here, but never mind. I point my phone and snap a few pics. "And that was caused by only water?"

"I get distracted. Someone knocked at the door, trying to sell me something, and next thing I knew there was water pooling out from under the bathroom door and it went on to soak the carpet in the hallway."

"But it was only water?" There's something about the stain that doesn't feel like it's only from good ole H_2O.

Her eyes widen as she bobs her head up and down with much enthusiasm. "I swear. Want to sit down for a minute and have a fresh-baked cookie?"

Things I could get used to, but not with the to-do list I'm currently being held accountable to. I shake my head as I snap a few more photos. "No, thank you. I wish I could, but I need to get back and take care of this with Levi."

"Tell you what, I'll pack one for you to go," she says as she heads into the kitchen. "You know, I did call Austin about this last month. Left a message. Actually, I left two. Never heard back. Isn't he supposed to be the person who we talk to?"

"He is," I say, bristling when I hear his name. "But with his recovery and his therapy schedule, it's better for the guys to have me stepping in now to help bridge the gaps."

As the twinge in my wrist sends me a little reminder of my encounter with Austin the day before, even I'm impressed with how politically correct I sound. Better than, "No. Do not talk to Austin. He is the devil. Lucifer. The king of Hades."

"That sweet boy has been through so much. I know he's busy; I see him over at the high school at least once a week working out with the kids there."

Do my ears perk up? You bet they do, especially when everyone around him seems to think he's a recluse. I trail into the kitchen behind her. "He goes to the high school?"

"I think it's him." Mrs. Rosenblatt plops a few cookies into a tiny sandwich bag and closes its special seal. Blue and yellow make green. "It looks like him, and his truck. I've never bothered to go look closer to see if it is. I just thought maybe, since he's busy working on his Achilles, he could be going there to lift his spirits."

Interesting. But not for me to unpack right now. I take the small parcel Mrs. Rosenblatt holds out to me and tuck it into my purse. "Thank you. I'm going to go so I can get these photos to the guys and we can get started on fixing this for you."

"That's lovely, thank you." She turns to me and holds out another couple of small bags of cookies. "Here. One for Levi and one for Austin, too. Can you pass them onto the fellas?"

Smiling, I take the other presents and add them to my bag. "Of course."

In a few minutes, I'm back out on the street and climbing in behind the wheel of my car. I want to get things rolling for this nice woman, so I dial Levi's number. I'm not at all surprised when it's sent right to voicemail. He'd mentioned, as had Georgie, that his schedule was crazy.

So, I man up and dial Georgie. That's right, I'm chicken. I know I'm working for the Porter boys, but Georgie is my security blanket. When it rings and rings and eventually goes to voicemail, I hang up and try again. Surely I am not going to have to do something I really don't want to do already, am I?

When I'm sent to voicemail, again, I can only hang my head. There's a flip in my stomach as I realize if I want to take care of this repair for this kind little old lady, I need to actually speak to Austin.

* * *

As I pull into the driveway, the gravel crunches beneath my tires, sounding louder than it should, like it's trying to remind me that turning back is still an option. I kill the engine and take a deep breath, letting the crisp evening air fill my lungs. The scent of damp earth and fallen leaves is almost too peaceful for what's ahead. I sit there for a beat longer, watching the sun dip below the horizon, like it's saying, *Good luck, Bex, you're gonna need it.*

The walk across the field is a mix of dread and determination. The cool grass brushes against my shoes, almost as if it's trying to trip me up before I get there. The distance between my place and Austin's feels annoyingly short, like the universe is conspiring to get me to his front door faster than I'd like. His porch light glows in the twilight, a beacon that says, *You're here now, no turning back.* Each step feels like I'm walking to my doom—or at least to a conversation I'd rather avoid. But here I am, crossing the field like a woman on a mission, even if that mission is just to survive another round with Austin.

In no time at all, I'm ascending the steps to his porch, giving myself a pep talk to end all pep talks, and I knock.

The door opens, but only a crack. You could barely even slide a piece of paper through it, but even I can tell there's a grown man on the other side glaring at me.

"What?" he growls.

I dangle the two packages of cookies in front of me as bribes. "Gifts for you and Levi. Courtesy of Mrs. Rosenblatt."

"You could have left it in the mailbox, you know."

There is something in his tone that I can't deal with any longer. I chuck the cookies at the door. "You know, I feel like you used to be nicer."

He blinks once, ignoring my comment. "What's going on that you can't text?"

Shaking my head, I quickly fill him in on my morning, pulling my phone out and showing him the photos—although, I have no clue how he's able to even see a thing through that tiny slit.

When I'm done with my spiel, I'm met with silence. Uncomfortable silence, at that. I can't even tell if he's still breathing or not.

"So," I begin, "should I make some calls, or is there a system in place for handling a complaint like this?"

I wait for what feels like several long, drawn-out minutes before he clears his throat. When he does speak, he's a bit softer. Not much, but enough.

"Honestly, I have no idea. I'd say defer to my brother."

"I tried that already."

"Have you tried Georgie?" he asks.

I nod. "She's busy. At least I think she is since she didn't pick up. Probably at her bookstore."

"You didn't think to go by and talk to her, then?"

This feels like the passing of the buck. I'm familiar with this system and I am not a fan. Especially when I'm dealing with a very privileged man who seems to have reality twisted.

"Why would I go by and bother her at her job when you're here, in your house, doing nothing?"

Austin opens the door only to glare at me as he pulls it back, wide, to gather momentum as he swings it shut.

But, in what will go down in the history books as the worst idea ever in the history of worst ideas, something inside me decides that now is the exact time I should take a stand.

As he goes to shut the door, with what I'm sure he thinks is going to be a resounding bang, I make a choice. A choice to stick my foot in the path of said door.

What a dumb idea.

As the heavy wood connects with the tiny bones in my foot, it's like a thousand fireflies have all decided to fan out across my line of vision at once, trying to dispel the feeling of pain and irritation that is coursing its way across my body, both electrifying and chilling me from the inside out at one time.

As I fall to the porch, silently screaming because there are no words, I can see the fear on Austin's face as he swings the door back open and drops to the floor with me.

"Oh my God," he says as he hits the ground, grabbing at me but not touching me at all. "I am so sorry…"

I hold up a finger, silencing him. "Do. Not. Talk."

"But," he sputters, his face filled with worry and concern, "why did you stick your foot back in the door?"

"Because I'm not done." I might throw up from the pain, but I've got something to say. I reach into my pocket and pull out a list and shove it in his direction. "I spent the morning stopping by the buildings Levi asked me to, and these are all the people I met and what they need. Seems that they haven't seen you around to talk to you about it in a long time. They need things."

His eyes pull from mine as he accepts the piece of paper, inspecting it. He casts his eyes across it, but drags his gaze back to meet mine.

"Are you okay, Bex?"

"I'm fine," I hissed, ignoring the dull pain and pointing to the list. "So, will you deal with this?"

"If I take care of these things, will you stop your dog from doing his business on my property?"

I do a double take with so much intensity, my neck almost breaks. "You can't be serious."

"I am," he says with a shrug.

"But she's not my dog," I say, throwing a hand in the air. "She?"

"Harley. That's what her tag says, at least I think it's a she, but see? I don't even know the dog's true gender."

60

He shakes his head. "I don't care."

"I do. I don't pay vet bills. Therefore, not mine."

"Well, you don't want to pay for her special 'treasures' to be picked up, do you?"

I fight the urge to scratch my head when he says this. Also, lest we forget, he just called a dog's number two a treasure. "Is there really a service for that?"

Austin rolls his eyes. Part of me thinks he's enjoying this. "Can you stand up?"

"Yes," I snap, planting my hands on the ground. I firmly push myself upward, only to wince in pain and fall to the ground again. "Well, I'll be able to soon-ish."

Austin points to my ankle. "May I take a look?"

My eyes almost roll into the back of my head. "Now you're a doctor?"

"I've had enough physical therapy and time on the field to know about an injury."

He has a point.

"Fine."

Oh-so-gingerly, Austin gently rolls up my pant leg, scrunching up the fabric to the top of my calf so he can look closer at my foot. He slowly begins pressing it, moving it in a circle, giving the blood a chance to flow again.

His touch is surprisingly warm and careful. As his fingers graze my skin, I feel a jolt of something unexpected—a strange mix of relief and surprise. It's as if his touch has a direct line to my nerves, sending a wave of comfort through me that I didn't anticipate.

He presses and prods with the expertise of someone who's had his share of injuries, but his touch is softer than I expected. Each movement is slow and deliberate, like he's trying to be as gentle as possible, and it's strangely soothing. For a moment, I forget about the pain in my ankle and focus on the warmth of his hand, the way his fingers are precise but tender.

"You know," I say, trying to mask my surprise with sarcasm, "if you start offering foot massages, you might just make a fortune."

He glances up at me, a smirk playing at the corner of his mouth. "I'll add it to my list of side hustles."

I catch his gaze and, for the first time, I notice how close we're sitting, how his hand is still resting on my ankle. There's an unexpected intimacy in the way he's caring for me, and it's disorienting. I wasn't prepared to feel this way—touched and cared for by someone who's clearly more than just a grumpy neighbor.

"Thanks," I say, my voice softer than I intended. "I didn't realize you were so... considerate."

Austin's eyes meet mine, and there's a flicker of something —maybe surprise, maybe amusement. "Well, don't go spreading it around," he replies, his tone light but sincere. "I've got a reputation to uphold." He looks back down at my foot. "There's no swelling, but you'll probably have a bruise and me saying I'm sorry to you for the rest of your life."

Before I can respond, he extends his hands toward me, his palms open and waiting. "Come on, let's get you up."

I blink, momentarily stunned by the gesture. It's not just the offer of help—it's the way his hands are reaching out, as if he genuinely wants to make sure I'm okay. For a second, I hesitate, caught off guard by the unexpected kindness.

"Well, look at you, all chivalrous and stuff," I say, trying to mask my surprise with a wry smile. "Next thing you know, you'll be rescuing cats from trees."

Austin chuckles, clearly amused by my reaction. "Considering I slammed your foot in the door, it's the least I can do."

I grasp his hands, and as he helps me up, I'm struck by how firm yet gentle his grip is. There's a strange comfort in his touch, a solidity that I didn't expect from someone who's been more of a grumpy neighbor than a knight in shining armor. He pulls me to my feet with surprising ease, and I find myself standing a little closer to him than I anticipated.

"Thanks," I mutter, still feeling the warmth of his hands on mine. "I didn't think you had it in you."

Austin shrugs, a playful smirk tugging at his lips. "Neither did I."

Rolling my eyes, I let my weight drop to my injured foot, surprised by how much better it's starting to feel.

Austin watches as I stand on both feet and get my balance back. "I can drive you back to your place if you don't want to walk."

"I'm fine," I lie through my teeth. Last thing I want is to be stuck in close proximity with this man. I'd rather army crawl across the field in a lightning storm with steel rods strapped to my back than for that to happen.

He nods. "Fine."

When I turn around, I put a little more weight on my foot, feeling pain searing through it. It's not broken, I know that much, but like he said, it's gonna leave a giant bruise. Squaring my shoulders, I start the slow and arduous task of getting down his porch steps when Austin pipes up one last time.

"So, do we have a deal? You're gonna keep that dog..."

Spinning around on my one good foot, I find him already back in the foyer and closing his door. I tilt my head to the side and plant a hand on my hip.

"Don't you find it silly to be arguing with me while hiding on the other side of the door? Kinda like being behind a hedge isn't it?"

Bull's eye.

"Leave my hedge alone and keep your dog off my land," he

growls, his eyes narrowing. "I don't want feces scattered everywhere."

Keeping my eyes locked with his, I make my way around the yard, breaking our gaze long enough so I can peek at the paddock in the back. Using my chin, I indicate the section where a large herd of cattle is grazing nearby. "Really?"

His lips pull into a taut line. "The owner of those guys pays me to have them poop on my property."

"So, because you're paying me, does that mean you're going to come and 'leave treasures' on my property?" You can bet I said this with my hands flying into the air and making a big show of using air quotes, too.

My big comeback. Sounded way better in my head.

Austin's lips twitch as he tries not to smile. "That's not what I meant, but hey, maybe I will. Could use some extra cash."

"You're unreal," I mutter, barely containing my frustration.

He shrugs with a smirk. "And you're a pain. But at least you're good for some entertainment."

"None of this is ideal," I snap, turning on my heel. "You've got the list. Go over it, and I'll check in tomorrow. Don't get too cozy with it—I've got better things to do than listening to your grumbling."

Austin chuckles, his voice trailing after me. "Sure thing, just don't get your foot caught in any more doors on your way out."

"Right," I call back, not looking over my shoulder. "I'll make a note to avoid your 'charming' company as well."

As I head back to my place, with a subtle limp of my own doing, I might add, I shake my head, half-amused and half-exasperated.

If dealing with him is this much of a circus, I might need to start selling tickets.

EIGHT

Austin

I t seems to me that the months I've spent sulking in what I thought was a cool closed-off solace has finally played its hand against me. Karma's visit was expected, but I never thought I'd be treated to all of her fury with me at one time. She's seeped in and I can't escape. That's right folks, she's moved in next door and is slowly making her way into my life, reminding me that there's a life out there I left behind.

And it *was* a good one.

As I push a slice of bread into the toaster this morning, I can admit that I could have been nicer last night. I'd just told my brother, my own flesh and blood, that I want to be more positive, and yet, the first chance I had to do it for Bex, I failed.

Throwing open the door to the fridge, I spy a container of lasagna left by Amy this morning as I reach for some butter and jelly. It's getting to the point where I need to call her employer, but not now. I'm having enough trouble getting through my own days, I don't want to add upset to someone else's. And when I finally do it and she finds out I'm letting her go, she's going to be unhappy.

An alarm on my watch sounds, reminding me that Emma

will be here soon for our Wednesday session. As I change into my workout gear, thoughts come on that I can't stop.

Did I spend last night in bed thinking about what a jerk I am? Perhaps mulling over the fact I should show up with a present of some kind to Bex's today? Although, I don't know what I could get for the most annoying neighbor ever—is there a tumbler for that?

The sound of something sizzling, followed by a loud pop and the smell of smoke pulls my attention to the toaster. My eyes land on it as a tiny plume of black smoke rises from its opening, the spot where my bread had just gone in, and I shake my head.

Great. I'm repelling small appliances now.

When I met Bex originally, which wasn't even that long ago, I was happy. I was better then, not this shell of who I used to be. I was Austin Porter, one half of the amazing NFL Porter Brothers duo, a tight end for the Tampa Bay Thunderbolts, who was on his way to the Hall of Fame if he kept things up.

Now, I'm Austin Porter, the guy with a limp and no team whose toaster just broke.

There's a hallway off the kitchen that I don't walk down if I can help it; it's lined with photos from my football days. From high school, to college, and then to the NFL. Mom, Levi, and Georgie had put them up after I moved in, an effort to surprise and motivate me. How were they to know it would only make my heart heavier?

"Hey, hey!" a familiar voice calls out as the back door slams closed. Emma is standing in my kitchen, grinning at me. And quite wickedly, too. "I just saw a man dressed as a dinosaur shove a bundle of what looked like envelopes in your mailbox. Is that odd?"

"No. That's Jared—he's a mailman by morning and one of those people who shows up for kids' parties by afternoon."

"Ah. And here I thought it wasn't normal." Emma sniffs the air. "Smells like something's burning."

I point to the toaster. "Breakfast."

"Good thing I brought this." She holds up a small bag, stamped with Red Bird Cafe on it. Treats from my favorite spot the next town over. These are treats usually reserved for bribery or asking for a favor.

Narrowing my eyes, I watch as she opens the bag and pulls out an apple fritter.

"Red Bird special of the day. Homemade, too." She waves it in the air, taunting me. "It's fall, y'all."

I want to play coy, but really I can't. "I never should have told you that cinnamon and sugar is my kryptonite."

"We all have something." She laughs, tossing the bag closer to me. "Plus, I wanted you to have something in your hand as I gave you the news."

The bite I'd taken suddenly tastes like cardboard on my tongue. "News?"

She nods, pulling a chair out at the table, indicating I do the same. "We need to have a talk."

I've not seen Emma since the other day, when the whole Porter family pile-up happened. As I park myself in a chair across from her, my stomach hitches. Could she be quitting because of how we acted? How I acted?

"Look, Emma, before you get started, can I say I am so sorry for the other day?" Better late than never, right?

"I've been around doing this for a few years now, Austin. I've seen athletes react in a lot of different ways, so don't go thinking you're special," she says with a wink as she pops another bite of fritter in her mouth. "At least not for this."

"Okay," I say as I play with my fritter. Its sugary stickiness has attached itself to my fingertips and I'm a little obsessed. "What's up?"

"Well, I was looking at your recovery timeline recently.

After your injury, you had surgery and we got started almost right after that, as soon as you could handle it."

Nodding, I allow myself the luxury of taking a bite of the apple fritter, and it is damn good. "Uh-huh," I manage in between bites, praying I don't start moaning with delight.

"Normally, it can take six to nine months for recovery, and longer depending on what sport an athlete like yourself wants to return to. Your doctors weren't sure if returning to the NFL was a possibility for you. Do you remember that?"

"Do I?" I interrupt myself with a chortle. "Of course I do. I think I stopped breathing that day."

"Sounds about right." She chuckles. "Well, I haven't said anything, but the last two weeks I've been putting you through extra tough drills, challenging you. Assessing you. I wanted to see for myself if you'd have any issues going back to football."

My jaw locks as I freeze in my place. Time stands still; in fact, I don't think I'm breathing.

"It's been almost eighteen months since you were injured. Well over a year that you've been doing therapy with me."

I slowly let out a breath of air, trying really hard to not let it go in a whoosh. I don't want Emma to know I'm literally holding my breath as she speaks. I want to grip the table and scream, "AND?" but I stay calm.

"The last test you scored really well in. Neuromuscular control. You've also done a range of movement and weight-bearing tests, but I disguised them as your exercises." She grins at me, pleased with herself. "The last thing you need to do is hop testing. I wanted to let you know that if you pass that this week—which I know you will—well, Austin Porter, get ready. Because I'll be able to recommend that you get back on the field ASAP."

If this were a Disney film, there would be birds in the air chirping, flying in a circle around my head. They would layer me with wreaths made of roses and lure me into the meadow to dance with them as the fireflies did their own choreographed show around us, like a thousand tiny fireworks displays going off at once in faerie land.

But it ain't Disney. This is Sweetkiss. So I do what I can do best: I stand up, throw my arms in the air, and scream as loud as I can.

"I DID IT!!!!!!"

Emma laughs, clapping her hands together. "Congrats, Austin. But also, play it cool, we have one more test."

I can hear the words, but it doesn't matter. There's a light at the end of the tunnel.

Finally.

* * *

Once our session was done, I spent the rest of my day working on homework and exercises Emma requested of me. She'd explained how the hop test would look and gave me some performance indicators I could work on on my own in preparation. She also asked me to add visualization to my daily routine, something I used to do for mindset work but had dropped to the wayside in my depression around my injury. I'd promised her I would. I want to pass this test as much as I'm sure she wants me to so she can move onto the next victim...I mean patient.

After winding down with an hour of yoga and fifteen minutes of meditation and visualization, I walk into the living room and settle in on the couch, fingering my phone. I could call my mom and tell her, or Levi. But I want to see their faces when I tell them. Part of me wants to call Bex and tell her I'm sorry for how I acted, but the part of me that has received good news knows better. I've managed to make her feel unwelcome, yell at her, accidentally splash mud all over her, and now I can add slamming her foot in my door to that list.

Oof. If I were an emoji, I'd be the guy slapping his forehead. What a horrible idiot I've been. But this is one idiot who is going to make things right. As these thoughts dance around in my mind, I realize she'd said she was going to check in with me today and hadn't, and she's the kind of woman who I feel is true to her word.

Looking around the room, I realize this may be a fortuitous opening so I can talk to her. In no time at all, I'm throwing a sweatshirt on and heading out the door. I have the whole walk across the field to think about my actions. At least I can try to start things from ground zero and not be such a jerk now, right?

Movement across the field to my right catches my eye. When I look, I spot a familiar four-legged creature, charging across the length of the field to make it back home.

"Is she really going to try to tell me that dog isn't hers?" I mutter, only to scold myself. That was the old Austin. The one who was reeling from his injury. This one, the one I want to be, isn't bitter. At least, that's how I was B.A.: Before Achilles.

When I knock on her door, I shouldn't be surprised that her dog is suddenly at my feet. Hanging out with me like we're old mates. I want to be right, to point to the animal and go "The dog's here, so the dog's yours!" but sometimes being right is really useless. I can't put my finger on it, but I get the distinct feeling that this is one of those times.

Something moves on the other side of the door. The back porch light comes on, blinding me. Bex opens the door, her line of sight falling to the dog beside me, licking his front right paw.

"I told you, he's not mine," she says with a sigh. "If

Grumpy Dwarf is angry with the sweet, stray dog, then he needs to talk about it with him. Not me."

With a roll of her eyes, she goes to close the door. But I'm fast and stick my foot in its path, giving her a taste of her own medicine.

She glares at my foot. "I'd be careful if I were you. I seem to owe you a door slam on *your* metatarsals."

Smirking, I point to my feet. "Steel-toe boots," I say as I let a huge grin take over my face. I feel like a Ringling Brothers clown.

She brings that glare up about six feet, slamming her eyes into mine. "As someone once said to me, what's going on that's so important you can't text?"

Sucks when your own words come back to bite you in the backside, doesn't it? "I deserve that."

Bex's eyes light up and she leans against the door frame, throwing the back of her hand against her forehead and feigning as if she's going to pass out. "I can't believe it. Your mouth to my ears."

I feel heat hitting my cheeks, embarrassment beginning to take over. Even though I want to hide, I came over here because I need to stop being a jerk and take responsibility for my actions. And I want to start with Bex.

"Look," I shove my hands in my pockets, trying to stuff away my own vulnerability. "I came over to apologize."

"For which part?" she asks, lips twisted in an evil smile. "The poop, the mud, the slamming of my foot in the door, making my life in my new house harder than it needs to be…"

"Okay." I hold up my hands as if I'm going to surrender. "I get it. I have a lot to say I'm sorry for, but I'm here. Saying I'm sorry."

"Are you just a boy standing in front of a girl asking her to love you?"

"Love? Who brought that up?" I didn't say a word about

feelings. It's like we skipped a line at the amusement park. "You got the wrong impression—"

She throws her head back and laughs, the evil sliding off her features as the German shepherd pushes its way past us and makes its way into her house. For a dog that's not hers, it looks really comfy moving around here.

"I was quoting a movie, goofball. *Notting Hill*." She stares at me, then steps back waving her hand with a flourish. "I'm boiling water for some hot tea. Why don't you come in and have a cup with me."

I've got options here. I could say no, take the time to apologize for all of my sins, then head home to...do what? Sit on my couch? Maybe make some dinner, maybe order takeout? I could call my mom and tell her what Emma said...

The other option is to follow this beautiful, feisty woman inside her home and have that cup of tea. Do what a part of me has wanted to do since I found out she was moving here: get to know her more.

The other option doesn't open me up to further disappointment, though. It's safe. It's how I like to play things and should play them so I can get back on the field as soon as possible. I mean, I can go back home now and make a list of all the things I need to do, like call my coach and see if he's still as keen on having me around as Levi said he was, then I can see how soon I can get back into practice.

But this option is more interesting. I'd like to think it has potential, at least it did when we first met, you know, "B.A."

I could go.

Or I could stay.

"So," she says, cocking her head to the side. "Tea?"

NINE

Austin

I stand in Bex's living room, my gaze wandering over the photos she's hung up on the wall. Each one tells a story—her life captured in moments of laughter, adventure, and the people who matter to her.

My eyes drift to the photos beside it, each one pulling me deeper into Bex's world. One is of her standing on a beach, the wind whipping through her hair as she laughs at something off-camera. The sun is setting behind her, casting a golden glow that makes her look almost ethereal, like she belongs in that perfect, carefree moment. The other photo shows her in a cozy bookstore, curled up in an oversized armchair with a book in hand, a contented smile playing on her lips. The warmth of the place seems to seep out of the image, making it easy to see why she loves it there. Each picture reveals a different side of her—a woman who finds joy in the little things, who's lived a life full of these quiet, beautiful moments.

But then, one photo stops me cold. It's Bex and Georgie, arms wrapped around each other, both smiling like they don't have a care in the world. They're at that game—*the* game where everything went sideways for me, where my Achilles snapped and my whole life flipped upside down. Seeing them so happy, completely unaware of what was about to happen, sends a jolt through me. It's like looking at a moment that's been etched into my life, only now with a connection to Bex that I never saw coming.

"Chamomile or peppermint?"

"Chamomile, please," I say, keeping my focus on the photos on the wall. The hall light flicks on above me and I turn around to find Bex standing with a mug in her hands.

"Here." She passes it to me. When I thank her, I notice how pale she is. I hadn't been able to tell before when we were outside, but now indoors and under this light, I can see she doesn't look well.

"Thank you," I mumble, watching as she walks away slowly. Her gait isn't the energetic, snappy one that I'm used to. I'd say she seems defeated, but that's a stretch. Tired maybe?

"I'm still quite curious why the evening visit, Austin," she says as she grabs a prescription pill bottle off the counter, opening it and popping a pill in her mouth. I'm both shocked and impressed when she swallows without any hydration. "Last time I saw you, I was plotting how to come back and destroy you, which I know sounds dramatic. You can bet I was at least trying to figure out how soon I can sue my new employer for injuries sustained on the job my first day."

"I know, I'm sorry." I take a sip of the chamomile tea, which is delicious, forgetting about her coloring for now. "I am. It's been a rough year. Actually, more than that, but that doesn't matter. What does matter is that I've been horrible to a lot of people. My family can handle it, but doing it to someone like you, or even Emma or Georgie..."

"Who's Emma?"

I really hope that's a little jealousy I'm detecting. "My

physiotherapist. She's had to deal with me being moody, but lately she's had to bear witness to my bad attitude with my family and she's gotten an earful or two about you as well."

"Wow." Bex folds her arms in front of her and smiles. "Guess I got under your skin."

"Guess so," I say, returning the smile. I keep my sights on her, watching as Bex steadies herself and closes her eyes, her right hand floating to her chest as she inhales sharply. "You okay?"

"Oh, my foot?" She flexes it. "It's sore, but I'm fine."

"No," I say as she rubs her chest again. "That."

"Palpitations," she whispers, opening her eyes slowly. It's only now that I can tell those usually bright hazel eyes are dulled. "I'm in the middle of having an onslaught of them and it's wiping me out."

"I thought you looked like you weren't feeling well." Concerned, I put the mug down on a table nearby and walk to her side. "Can I do anything?"

She shakes her head. "I have an auto-immune disease and it likes to rear its head at inopportune times. This is one of them."

Bex pulls out a chair at her kitchen table and gently lowers herself into it, with what I can only describe as a relieved breath of air escaping her lips as she does. She closes her eyes again and sits still.

"It's Graves' disease," she says after a few moments of silence. Well, except for the sound of that dog in the other room scratching itself. I can hear the tags jingle on its collar, the sound of metal on metal swaying through the air and reverberating around us.

"Okay," I respond, pulling out a chair and sitting down myself. "That sounds..."

"Horrible, right?" She laughs, her eyes flicking open. "It's the worst name for a disease ever. People always think I'm dying when I tell them, but lucky for me I'm not."

"Noted." I watch as she takes a few more deep breaths. "But you are okay?"

She waves a hand in the air. "It's fine. I have an overactive thyroid, so it likes to work at a fast speed."

"Have you had it for a long time?"

"Ten years, maybe eleven?" She shrugs. "I was diagnosed after a really hard and stressful stretch of time in my life. I was losing a lot of weight but eating well over my calorie allowance, had hair falling out, anxiety was through the roof. Oh my gosh, don't even get me started on the brain fog. I was a multi-tasker who could spin plates and platters while tap dancing if I needed to, but that's no more."

"I had no idea," I start to say, and she interrupts with laughter.

"How were you supposed to know? It's not like we had time to talk or get to know each other."

"To be fair, you also don't look..." As soon as the words are about to fall off my lips I want to take them back. Shove 'em right in my mouth and forget I thought them.

"I don't look sick?" she says with a guffaw. An actual guffaw—then she sighs the heaviest sigh I think I've ever heard. "That's what most folks say to people like me and it's super annoying."

"I know." I groan. This quick visit to say I'm sorry is going downhill fast. "Can I add that to my list of things I'm sorry for?"

"It's becoming a long list, Austin," she manages with a wry smile.

"I can handle it," I retort.

"No doubt you can." She chuckles. "Not to change the subject, but did you call those people?"

"Not yet, but I will. I'm going to do it tomorrow." When

she looks at me with a stern expression, I reach over to pat her hand. It was meant to be a kind gesture, albeit pandering, but the moment my skin touches hers, I freeze. The softness of her hand surprises me as I feel the roughness from the callouses on the tips of my fingers as they catch on it. So smooth and soft, a suppleness that's telling of how she takes care of herself. The opposite of the guy who sits in front of her.

There's a moment where I want to let my fingertips trace their way across the back of her hand, allowing them to dance up her arm, but I stop myself. I snap my hand back, feeling the cold in the air as I do. Which is going to happen when you step away from the sunshine, isn't it?

"Trust me," I say as I clear my throat. "I am going to call all of them. I heard you yesterday. I've been absent and I need to show up more. In all ways."

Her mouth opens, her jaw slack as she watches me with a look I'd describe as judgmental curiosity. "Okay. So, this apology tour you're on. You serious?"

"Yes," I say, smacking my hands on the table and drumming my fingers. I have no idea how much time has passed since I arrived on her doorstep, but I'm liking the fact that I have no clue. That time is standing still and it's not just me. Or her, alone, in her house across the field.

It's us.

"Okay," she says, throwing her hands in the air. "I'm not going to question it anymore. I'll just say thank you."

"Thank you?"

"And you're forgiven."

My eyes almost jump from their sockets. "It's that easy with you?"

"Yes," she responds, looking at me quizzically. "Should it be harder?"

"Well, no, but..."

"Austin, do us both a favor and let it be okay."

The fact it's so easy for her to forgive and move on fills me with a feeling that's foreign, one that I'd forgotten until this moment. It's hope.

I turn my attention back to her. "How are you feeling now?"

She shakes her head. "I should go lie down."

"Do you have a doctor we can call?"

"I haven't had a chance to find one locally, at least not yet. But I saw my endocrinologist before I left LA. He reminded me that moving can cause a ton of stress and since I'm still getting my symptoms under control, I need to make sure I steer clear from as much stress as I can." She smirks. "Because that is so easy to do."

Laughing, I push my chair back and get up from the table. I hold out my hand for Bex to take. "Let's get you to the couch."

She eyes my hand for a moment before sliding hers on top of it. It feels nice to hold someone close like this, even if it is only the skin of our palms touching. For good measure, I wrap an arm around her waist to help guide her as we start our way across the room together.

When I get her to the couch, she literally pours onto it, falling over and landing on her side. She pats the top of the couch and I follow her path, seeing a blanket just out of her reach. Grabbing it, I snap it open and cover her with it as I kneel beside her.

"What do you need?"

She shakes her head. "Nothing right now. Just to chill out, I think."

"Are you sure?"

"Wow, when you come back from being a turd, you are Austin 2.0, aren't you?" She rolls over and faces me as she pulls the blanket up under her chin. "I'm okay. When you get diagnosed with Graves you have a choice to get your thyroid removed or not. I decided not to, so I took the chance that I could have to deal with this every now and then."

And here I've been sitting in my farmhouse feeling sorry for myself.

"Okay, well..." I scan the room, my eyes landing on the TV remote in the center of her coffee table. "How about I put on a movie for you?"

"A movie for us?"

"Us?"

She nods, eyeing the dog who is now curled up on the floor beside her. "Yes. Us. Me and Harley."

"I knew it."

Her lips twist as she fights a smile. I'm starting to realize I like that she smiles so much. I've not had this much goodness and sunshine in my world in a long time. Or maybe I haven't been open to letting it in. Until now, that is.

"If you're going to find a movie, *Notting Hill* pops to mind...if you're going to stay to watch it, that is."

"I can stay for a bit," I acknowledge, pressing the power button as I land in the recliner next to her sofa. Don't want to appear too eager, but let's be honest: this is the closest I've come to a night out in a long time. I press a few more buttons, find the movie on one of her streaming services, and hit play.

In no time, I'm pulled in. Immersed in a neighborhood in London where Hugh Grant and his salty roommate make everything okay. Bex, who had been laughing away as well, has gotten quiet. I glance over, thinking she's probably simply lost in the movie, but then I notice the steady rise and fall of her chest. Her eyes are closed, her breathing slow and even. She's asleep.

For a moment, I just watch her—taking in the way her lashes rest against her cheeks, the slight parting of her lips, how peaceful she looks. Something tightens in my chest, a feeling I can't quite name but that I know means trouble. It's like I've been hit with a realization I didn't see coming, and suddenly, the world feels different.

"Nope," I mumble to myself, shaking it off as I grab my phone and sneak out to the porch, dialing our family doctor. It's after hours, but that's the good thing about small towns and personal connections. If the doctor knows you, he's going to chat with you.

Dr. Bloomfield picks up on the first ring. "Austin, everything okay?"

"I'm well, but I have a question about a friend who isn't if you have five minutes?"

"Of course. What's going on?"

I quickly run through what Bex has shared with me, while also expressing my concern. Dr. Bloomfield listens, clicking his tongue on the roof of his mouth. It's a sign of his thinking when I'm done talking.

"Honestly, Austin, it sounds like she knows what she's doing. She's calming herself when she feels her symptoms ramping up, and she's taking medicine. Unless she's got a fever or is experiencing symptoms that make her think a thyroid storm is evident, then she's good for now."

I understand what he's saying, but it doesn't change the fact I'm worried. I'd go so far as to say I'm scared, but I'm supposed to be the tough one here. "So, she's okay?"

"From what you've told me, yes. Graves is complicated, but it is treatable and can be addressed in a myriad of ways depending on the patient and the doctor. Let her lead you with this, and know she's fine. Graves is complicated. Okay?"

The sound of someone in the background talking to him reminds me that this man is at home and he's done me a huge favor taking this time to listen. I say a quick thank you, hang up, and then fire off an email to remind myself to call his office in the morning. Dr. Bloomfield won't bill me for that time, but that doesn't mean I can't pay him.

I let myself back inside Bex's house, closing the door quietly behind me as I enter the kitchen. Harley must have heard me as she jogs in with her ears perked up, watching me with those soulful, questioning eyes. I give her a quick scratch between the ears as I walk past, heading back to the living room.

Julia Roberts and Hugh Grant light up the flat screen, their banter filling the cozy space. I look around, taking in the warmth of the room, the way it feels like home. Then my gaze lands on Bex, curled up on the couch, fast asleep. Her soft breathing is the only sound other than the movie, and that little smile still lingers on her lips, even in sleep. I feel a warmth spread through me, something solid and sure.

This—being here, with her—feels right in a way I can't fully explain.

I could get used to this.

TEN

Dex

When I open my eyes, sunlight streams through a break in the curtains. Squinting, I let my vision come into focus, searching my memory for when I pulled the curtains. But the curtains don't look like mine. Mine are rose-colored and long...or at least I thought they were.

Slowly, the realization hits me that I'm not in my apartment in LA, but waking up on the couch in my new house in North Carolina. I take a moment to look around, my heart doing a little patter when I spot Harley on the floor curled up next to someone who looks like...Austin?

I sit up and take a big breath, and also a moment to close and open my eyes again. So, last night really happened. Austin's here. That wasn't a dream. He came over to apologize, and judging by the way his arm is curled around Harley, he stayed for the puppy cuddles.

Austin's body is turned my way, his eyes closed and his chest moving with each breath he takes, while I sit here wondering if I'll get Dr. Jekyll or Mr. Hyde when he gets up. Shrugging the blanket off my body, I swallow a laugh. The irony. The injured player comes over to say he's sorry and ends up taking care of the person he's been mean to.

The reminder of the way I felt yesterday isn't a distant thought, but it helps that I'm feeling better today. I'm so used to this, it's honestly no skin off my nose. I know I stressed myself out and pushed myself too far, and now I need to pull it back. The move has happened, I've got a job. I just need to make sure I have peace around my home and then I'll feel like I've conquered the trifecta.

Austin begins to stir, his eyes fluttering open as he snaps them in my direction. If I'm not mistaken, those big, deep blue eyes of his are actually sparkling this morning.

"Hi."

"Morning." Standing up, I toss the blanket on the back of the couch. "Want some coffee?"

"Sure," he says as Harley stretches out even longer beside him, burrowing into his body even further. "I'd get up to make it for us..."

"No, please. Stay with that horrible beast," I say with a giggle. I stroll into the kitchen and brew a carafe of coffee for us, and take the time to pull a few pieces of fruit out and some muffins I'd picked up at the store the other day. In a few minutes, I'm back in the living room setting up our morning nourishment on the coffee table.

"Thanks," Austin says as he takes a sip.

"I'm usually not this together. You got lucky," I tease. I point to the pre-packaged muffins. "As you can see, they're homemade."

He holds it up and looks at it closely, turning it around in his hand. "Hey, you bought it, it's yours. You can call it what you want."

I hold my mug in the air and toast him. "Hear, hear."

This feels easy.

Austin pops one of the mini-muffins in his mouth and grins. "I was going to sneak out before you woke up."

"And leave me here wondering if your visit was my imagination?"

"Pretty much. Actually, the movie pulled me in and I needed to stay and see how Hugh would get the girl."

Laughing, I allow myself to sink back into the couch cushions. "Did you like the ending?"

"I did, but I was falling asleep." His eyes slide down to Harley, who has taken to a downward dog pose as she wakes up for the day herself. "And this one started shaking and would only stop if I was here with my hand on her body and petting her back. So I figured I was helping both of you if I stayed and kept Harley calm."

I don't miss that his mouth twitches as he says it. Biting my lip, I put my mug down while keeping an eye on him.

"Needless to say, last night was unexpected."

"Yeah, I feel like I caught you with your guard down?"

"Pretty much. If I hadn't been feeling so awful, I probably wouldn't have let you in—but I guess I was feeling generous," I tease.

"I'm glad you were," Austin acknowledges with a dip of his head and his eyes locked with mine. There's something so simple and easy in this moment, as if there's a lot being said yet no words dare happen, nothing verbal. Our only communication is our energy and a look.

I'm getting lost in the confusion I'm feeling around this not-quite-awake moment we seem to be having, so it's no wonder that when his phone suddenly dings I almost jump out of my skin.

"Sorry," Austin says with a chuckle as he grabs his phone from the table. He glances at the screen and furrows his brow as he goes to stand up. "Give me a second, I need to make a call real quick."

"Sure," I say as he disappears into the kitchen. I hear the door open and close as he lets himself outside, Harley hot on his heels.

Sitting alone, I can unravel a little more of what happened yesterday. Right?

Only the more I try to reflect, the more opposition my mind gives me. It's like it's got whiplash, which I can fully understand. We've gone all over the place with this guy from war to kindness to...well, jury is still out.

I can see Austin pacing the yard from my spot and it makes me smile; there's a delicious ease in the way he moves, his muscular frame silhouetted in the sunshine with a dog on his heels as he paces, focusing on whoever is on the other end of his call.

To me, being around Austin is like biting into one of those chocolate hard shells you pour over ice cream. It's a little odd, almost jarring—the way it's hard and crusty, not smooth and warm like fudge. You expect something sweet and rich, but instead, you get this cold, stiff exterior that takes a bit of effort to crack through.

However, once you do break through, there's something underneath that's worth it. The softness isn't warm, though—it's still ice cold, just like the ice cream inside. Maybe that's not the perfect comparison, because while the shell might be cold, there's something about discovering that softer side of him that makes you want to keep digging deeper, to see if there's warmth hiding somewhere after all.

The door closes in the kitchen, signaling Austin's return. But so does Harley, who comes running in and throws herself next to me, panting, with a tennis ball in her mouth.

I point to the ball as Austin comes into the room. "Where did you get that?"

He shrugs. "It was on the driveway. Maybe she brought it with her?"

I look at Harley, and Harley looks back at me with big brown eyes. "Well, at least you brought your own toys."

"Be careful, she may see Jared pull up wearing one of his costumes and think he's a giant squeaky toy," Austin says with a laugh.

"Good point," I agree. "But, since she's not my dog, I probably don't need to worry about that."

Austin grins. "Probably."

I head into the kitchen, taking my mug with me and grabbing Austin's empty one as I go. "More coffee?"

"Please," he says as he follows me. "I had to slam mine during that call."

"Good news?" I ask. Not that I expect him to share it with me, considering we were at each other's throats a mere twenty-four hours ago.

"It was my coach, Coach Donovan from Tampa Bay. Looks like I'm going back to practice soon."

Now there's a surprising bit of information. "You are?"

"Before I came over last night, I found out that I'm one assessment away from being allowed to train again for the team."

"Really?" I put the coffee pot down in mid-pour and stare at him blankly at first as his words sink in, then I clap my hands together in excitement. "That's amazing! You've got to be so thrilled."

"When Emma told me, I was thrilled. I was so surprised I didn't know what to do, but I wanted to tell someone." He shakes his head. "But then all I could think about was the fact I'd been so rude to you. To everyone around me. It made me question the karma of it all, how I was getting the good end of the stick, you know?"

I go back to pouring our coffee, then handing him his mug. "Austin, you were sidelined from a horrific injury and it sounds like you have been beating yourself up and doing that thing people do to themselves where they blame their actions for all the things wrong in the world."

He takes the mug from me and leans against the counter. "What do you mean?"

"Look, I've worked with extreme achiever personalities—what else would you get in LA when you're dealing with actors and billionaires and all that jazz? You're an athlete, you are your craft. Much like an actor is. When things go wrong, you blame yourself and only you, and then those around you mistake your passion for venom."

"But I *was* being venomous," he pipes up. "That's why I came over here. I wanted to take accountability for how I've acted. I can do that with my family, and I will, but I don't know. For some reason yesterday it was more important that I make things right with you first."

"I appreciate that, and it's a good thing you did. It would seem I needed your help at the same time last night, so..." I smile and head back into the living room. "It's a win-win."

"I guess so," he says with a chuckle as he settles into my recliner. "You're very forgiving. Should I be worried? Am I going to go home and secretly, while I've been here, you've had a thousand pounds of cattle crap dumped in my living room?"

"Now that would be a great prank, but no." I snort. "I'm not that organized nor that vindictive. But the mud splatter-ing...yeah, you pushed me with that one."

"I feel like I'll be apologizing to you for a long time," he says, wincing.

"At least as long as we live next to each other." I snap my fingers. "Don't forget, you need to call those tenants today. Just let them know I spoke to you and that you're aware of the issues. If they hear your voice and know things are in the works, everyone will calm down."

"Which means Levi will calm down, too," he says with a grin.

"Exactly."

"I will." He looks at his watch and starts as he does. "It's almost ten? I need to get going."

I watch as he jumps up and heads into the kitchen, looking around. "I know I took my shoes off..."

"I saw them in there," I call out as I hop up and join him. I point under the dining table. "There."

Austin slips his shoes on and then looks out the window that faces his house and the hedge. "Man, you really don't have a view because of that hedge, do you?"

"You're so observant." I grab his coat and shove it his way. "Unless we want to ruin this call for peace, you should get out of here before we start arguing about the hedge."

"I don't have time for that today." He grips the door handle and looks at me. "Thank you for letting me in last night, Bex. I am going to be different. Not just try to be, I will be, but I just ask that you give me some grace while I figure it out. After all, we're working closely together now and we live..." He rolls his eyes. "I don't have to tell you where we live."

"No, you don't." I nod toward his truck. "You'd better go. And brush those teeth first, too, you hear me?"

Do I delight when his mouth drops open? Not then, but when his hand flies to his mouth so he can do a breath check, that's when I giggle.

"Go. And let me know what happens with the tenants, okay?"

He gives me a salute as he jogs out the door and heads to his truck, leaving me in a swirl of confusion. Like dealing with Clark Kent when you find out he's Superman.

Who was that guy?

I don't have to think about it too long; my phone, which is in the living room, starts chiming, signaling a call. It's an unknown number, but I'm feeling like throwing caution to the wind today and pick it up while Harley threads herself in and out of my legs.

"Hello?" I manage in between pats on Harley's back.

"My name is Felicity and I'm the pet sitter for Harley. I picked up a message this morning that she's been coming to your place?"

I eye Harley, my stomach dipping. "Yes, she's right here now, in fact. Stayed here last night."

"Oh man, that dog. She keeps running away, but it sounds like she keeps coming just to your place." The woman sighs heavily in my ear. "I'm so sorry, if you tell me your exact address, I'll come over and get her now."

I rattle off my address and fight the sadness inside. I mean, I wanted to find Harley's owner so they could be reunited, but why does it have to hurt my heart to give her back?

"Great," Felicity says. "I'll be over soon. That dog. To be honest, I'm not sure she even likes her owners."

"What makes you say that?"

"She never listens to them when they give her commands, but she listens to me. I've been working with her more on her training while her people are away looking at homes in Florida. They're moving soon, so I'm on a time crunch to get her more obedient."

"I guess with her sneaking over here it's not helping." I ruffle Harley's fur, letting my fingers dig into its thickness. "Well, we'll be here."

I hang up, a fleeting wave of depression washing over me. I knew this was a possibility, but at least Harley reminded me that I love dogs like I do. And it's a mystery now solved. I know the dog's name, gender, and the story of the owners.

I let my eyes wander, looking out the window toward Austin's.

One mystery solved, now there's only one more to go.

ELEVEN

Austin

Sitting in the parking lot outside of the gym where my brother is a member, I begin to question my being here. I'd gone to great lengths to find out from Georgie via text last night where he'd be this morning, and now I'm feeling like a right stalker.

Glancing at the binoculars in my lap, I can't blame myself either.

My fingertips drum the steering wheel and I tap my foot to the beat. She said he goes in around nine-thirty and is out by eleven at the latest. I'd made sure to show up at ten-thirty. I'd even circled the parking lot to make sure his car was here, and I was rewarded. Now I wait.

I'd spent part of the time on the phone, calling a few of the tenants like Bex asked me to do. She was right: the three people I'd managed to chat with, including Mrs. Rosenblatt, were all happy to hear from me. From leaky faucets to updates on grandchildren, I was treated to a gamut of life news. And for once, I didn't mind it not being all about me.

Something flashes in the corner of my eye, pulling my attention toward the gym entrance as the door is closing. It's

Levi, walking across the lot with his head down and looking at his phone.

"Hey," I call out, sticking my head out the window of my truck. "What are you doing?"

Levi stops, staring at me like I'm an alien who just landed in front of him in a spaceship. "What are you doing here?"

"Stalking you." I shake my head and then start nodding as I hold up my binoculars. "No, really, stalking you."

"Okay," he says, swinging his duffle bag over his shoulder as he sashays up to my truck. "Why?"

"I'm on an apology tour."

"Like that TV show Mom used to watch—*My Name is Earl*?"

"Good show."

"Best. Seriously. Is that why?"

"I wanted to see if you'd throw a football with me."

I swear Levi stops breathing. "Of course...but—"

"Will you get in my truck?"

"We're good, right?" he asks as he takes the first step.

"We're fine. We've been fine since our call the other day. More than fine, really." I push my fingers through my hair. "Just get in. I want to show you something."

"And toss a ball?" he asks, walking around to the passenger door.

I wait until he's in the car and belted in.

"Maybe."

* * *

"You've been coming here every week for months to work out with the high school team?" Levi stares at me incredulously.

Our old alma mater. The one place I found safety, besides my house, for the last year.

"Yep," I say, grabbing a football from the sack by the

benches. We'd arrived just as the kids were wrapping up their morning drills, the coach recognizing my truck as we pulled in. "I started by coming and being their waterboy. I was desperate to get out of the house."

"Desperate?" Levi laughs. "I thought you were a recluse."

"I thought I was going to turn into one, and I didn't want to." I take the ball and hold it in the air. "Go long."

Levi jogs away and I let the ball go, watching it spiral perfectly through the air as he catches it with ease. Grinning, he holds the ball high.

"Good one. Like you've not been gone at all." He tosses it in the air and catches it. "Want me to throw it back?"

I point about fifty feet ahead of me with a grin. "Throw it that way."

Levi tilts his head, giving me a doubtful look. "You sure?"

"Trust me," I reply, getting into position with my heart pounding. As soon as he releases the ball, I'm off like a shot. I can feel the wind whipping past me, my feet barely touching the ground as I sprint toward my target. I push through the familiar but dull and lessened ache of my Achilles injury, feeling more alive than I have in months. The ball arcs high against the clear sky, a perfect spiral of orange and white against the backdrop of autumn leaves.

The world narrows to just me and that descending ball. Time seems to slow as I stretch out my arms, eyes locked on the ball. I position myself perfectly underneath it, and with a satisfying thud, I catch it, cradling it against my chest.

Levi's cheers pierce through the air, his voice echoing with excitement as he jumps and pumps his fist. "Holy...DUDE!" He dashes over to me, eyes wide with amazement. "What just happened?"

I quickly fill him in on the good news I'd gotten from Emma, along with the update from my coach that I could get back to practice once I'd passed the last assessment, and we high-five.

Levi shakes his head. "You're like a phoenix rising from the ashes, you know that?"

"Having a family that is as supportive as you guys has helped." I slug his arm. "Patient, too."

"We all have our moments, yours was just extended," he says, slugging me back.

"I've got a lot of making up for my actions to do."

"You will. Go easy on yourself. You've been through a lot." He tilts his chin down and stares in my direction. "And Bex? How are you two going to work together?"

"We'll be fine," I say easily. Maybe a bit too easily; Levi's eyebrows shoot up and almost pop off his head.

"I thought, in your own words, you wanted to kill each other?"

"Kill may be harsh," I say, waving a hand in the air. "I think we disagree on some things, but we'll be able to get along for the sake of having peace in Sweetkiss Creek."

Levi eyes me. "Uh-huh."

"What?"

He lifts a shoulder and lets it drop. "Remember Lacy Daily?"

"My middle-school girlfriend?"

"Yep. The one you were mean to. All the time. You would make fun of her, pull her hair. Anything to get a rise out of her so you had her attention."

"That's not the way I remember it, but go on."

He smirks, shaking his head. "You were relentless, man. The classic case of a kid not knowing how to deal with his feelings. But everyone knew you had a thing for her, even if you didn't. It was like you couldn't stand the thought of her not thinking about you, so you made sure she did."

I rub the back of my neck, the memory of those awkward

school days coming back in flashes. "I guess I wasn't as smooth as I thought."

"Smooth? You were about as smooth as sandpaper." He laughs. "But it worked, didn't it? She noticed you, all right. Probably still remembers you, too."

"What are you saying, Levi?"

"There are some similarities here." He bobs his head from left to right, as if mulling something over. "Lots of similarities. Like, a good amount. The teasing, the false 'no' and saying you can't stand her..."

"Stop it." I karate chop the air with my hand. If we're going to dig into my love life, I need a therapist here for that unraveling. "I'm not even going to entertain the thought with you."

"Fine, fine." Levi holds up his hands, then he looks around, nostalgia washing across his features. "We played some great games here."

"We qualified for State Champs in this stadium," I remind him.

"We sure did." He claps my back. "If I remember correctly, you went into the state championship game injured, didn't you?"

"I did," I say with a chuckle. "Good memory."

"You stepped on a mousetrap, right?"

I wince at the pain even now. "I thought my toe was going to need to be amputated." Okay, maybe I do have a flair for the dramatic.

"Please. It was barely sprained, though the newspapers made a big deal out of it."

"True," I say, nodding. "I think they called me the comeback kid."

"They sure did." He puts me in his sights. "Have you got one more in you?"

Grinning, I don't answer. Instead, we start walking in

unison back to the truck. From here, we return to the gym parking lot where I drop off Levi. I don't want to talk about my injury or future anymore, not now. And I know he's tired of hearing about it. He hops out and we promise to connect later, and I head home because I've got more calls to make.

The ride home is a bit more bubbly and jubilant than other times. I turn the dial to a local radio station that only plays pop music and let myself be lulled into my own carpool karaoke when Katy Perry comes on.

I'm not even embarrassed when a carload of teens pulls up next to me at a stoplight in town and catches me singing at the top of my lungs.

I'm back.

TWELVE

The smell of chai fills the air. Closing my eyes, I take a giant whiff of my drink. I'd treated myself to a latte on the way home after spending the morning with Mrs. Rosenblatt. Who knew one woman would have so much trouble trying to pick out a new color of carpet for her apartment?

The week has been surprisingly productive. Since Austin's sudden "come to Jesus" moment (a term that my new friend, Eric the landscaper, taught me), life has been so much easier. The song "Lovely Day" is stuck on repeat in my head simply because it fits.

Even Pearl, whose kitchen had caught on fire a few weeks ago and was still seething over Austin's lack of help, was beginning to thaw. The first time I met her, she'd let me know for several minutes how disappointed she was with him, making sure I was aware that she could have moved anywhere else in town but wanted to live in her particular apartment because the Porter boys always seemed so kind. But Austin's actions had upset her to no end.

Fast forward to today. I dropped by to touch base and make sure she's ready for her new oven and stove to be put in next week, and she's waiting with a bouquet of flowers to thank me for having Austin call her. Apparently, their conversation had been a good one.

Do I pat myself on the back? Maybe a little. Can't lie, it makes me happy to hear he's showing up. Like he owes me anything, which he doesn't, but the fact he's doing it for himself and the flow-on means his family is happy, well, that makes me happy.

The sound of an engine idling nearby lets me know that Jared's here. I peek out the window and find Aladdin tiptoeing up to the mailboxes. He hangs out for a moment, most likely just doing his job, but then his head snaps up and he looks over my way suddenly. Busted.

My hand lifts in the air on its own, like it has a string attached to it and there's a puppeteer somewhere making it move. Aladdin/Jared waves back, then does a leap in the air before he skips back to his car and takes off.

I don't think I'll ever get used to this. Part of me hopes I never do.

Smiling, I grab my notepad off the counter and look over my to-do list. I'm ticking my way through it. I've spoken to the tenants I need to, organized workmen, and emailed a list of what's happening to both Austin and Levi, plus I managed to get my own HVAC unit sorted out. That will go in next week, too.

There's only one name left on my list: Eric the landscaper. I drag my eyes toward the window, looking out at the hedge beyond. What am I going to do? On one hand, I have every right to do what I want. On the other hand, I have a neighbor I'm getting along with now. A neighbor who is my boss. I'd prefer not to rock the boat if I can help it.

But Eric is coming back over this week and he wants to know…will it stay or will it go?

I peer across to Austin's house and see the red truck

parked in the drive, along with a Toyota Tercel that appears every few days. I hate bothering anyone when they have company, but I need to deal with this and see if we can find some kind of compromise in the hedge.

Opening the door, I'm greeted by Harley, who pushes her way past me and saunters into the living room, plopping down on the floor near the fireplace.

"Come on in, why don't you?" I say with a laugh, shaking my head as I close the door behind me and head across the field. I've not left Harley alone in there before, but something tells me she'll be fine.

In no time I'm in front of Austin's door, knocking away. I'm a little surprised when a pretty blonde with perfect makeup, in perfect shape, and wearing her hair pulled up into a cute little bun on top of her head opens the door.

"Can I help you?" she asks, perkiness dancing on each word.

I start to open my mouth, but I'm interrupted.

"Hey, Bex," Austin says. I peek over her shoulder and find him standing in the hallway behind her grinning. He looks at the blonde. "Amy, this is Bex, my neighbor and also a colleague of mine. Bex, meet Amy. She's my house cleaner."

Amy grimaces slightly at the introduction, and I find myself admiring her makeup—which also makes me question how many house cleaners out there put on full makeup glam, as if they were getting ready to debut on a television show, to go to work? Granted, there are some who will, and good for them, but add in the perfectly pressed white shirt and the linen pants she's wearing and I'm beginning to doubt this woman is really a cleaner of any kind.

"Nice to meet you," I say as I step inside the doorway and angle past. I point to Austin. "I'm here to see that guy."

"Hmmm." She grunts, narrowing her eyes as she steps out of the way.

Austin, who has been watching Amy, slides his gaze over to me. "What's up?"

"Should I have texted?" I tease.

"No, I think we're past that, don't you?" he says with a grin. "I'm in here putting a bookshelf together. Come on, you can read the instructions to me while we talk."

"Sure."

I follow him down the hall and to a back room. It's empty except for various pieces of an Ikea bookshelf that are scattered here and there, with a piece of paper left sitting on top of the pile.

"So." I point to the mess on the floor. "This is our project?"

"Project is a loose term here. Gives more credit than I should get," he says. "I'm not good at Ikea anything. I ordered it and thought it would come already put together."

"Aren't you cute?" I tease, shaking my head as I hold my hand out. "I'm an Ikea pro. Hand me the Allen wrench and the paper, I'll have this baby put together in less than ten minutes."

He looks at me with wide eyes. "No way."

"Way."

He reaches into his pocket and pulls out his wallet. "I bet you dinner that you can't do it in ten."

"I love a challenge," I say as I crack my knuckles. "Accepted."

Taking the paper from his hand, I wait for him to give me the signal that the time is starting before I dive in. I was serious when I said I'm a pro at this; I used to live ten minutes away from an Ikea in LA, and for the first twelve years of my life there, I was a weekly regular at that store. I loved walking it and seeing new things, sitting on the uncomfortable couches, and randomly having some Swedish meatballs.

I can tell by Austin's stance that he doubts me. It's fine.

I'm used to people doubting me; it makes the look on their face when I win that much sweeter. And I'm not going to tell him that not only did I have this exact bookcase in my old place, but I also put two together for Spencer, so I know what I'm doing.

With two minutes left on the clock, I toss the wrench to the ground and clap my hands as I stand up.

"Time!" I scream as Austin laughs.

"You've got to be kidding me!" He cracks up and shows me my time. "A little over eight minutes. You're a mad genius."

I swat at him, but he puts his hand up as if he's about to stop me only to grab my arm, and we freeze. There's a moment where I could awkwardly pull away and change the subject, but there's another moment here. The one where I stay my ground and keep my eyes on his, and instead of stepping away, I do the opposite—I step toward him.

He drags his eyes slowly to my lips, heat flooding my body as he does. I don't know where my head's at, but I'm suddenly overly conscious of them—do they look smooth? I can get the worst chapped lips. It would be a crying shame if today was the day they start peeling. Also, gross, but just...not now.

I do a quick check and am pleased to report they feel fine. Smooth. In the process, though, I run them together slowly, forgetting that he is looking directly at them.

Now my overthinking comes into play. Does he think I'm rubbing my lips together for him? Does he want me to be? Maybe he thinks I'm being too forward, but I'm not—I was just making sure my lips at least look nice. No one wants to have a view of crusty lips, right?

"Hey," Austin whispers, his hand still wrapped around my forearm as he steps closer. "You look like you just spun out into a million different places. You okay?"

"Yeah," I begin to say, but then I stumble over my words.

"Or no. Maybe. Yes. Maybe. I am maybe okay. Definitely, maybe."

Austin lifts an eyebrow. "Definitely, maybe okay?"

"That's it," I say, taking a step closer to him. I can smell his aftershave. Spicy. Warm and invigorating, with notes of clove, cinnamon, and maybe a hint of pepper.

It's masculine and makes something inside of me ignite. I drag my eyes back to his again, making sure he's watching me, only this time when I glide my tongue across my bottom lip, I do it because I want to. Because I know he's watching, and I want him to see.

I watch as Austin's eyes suddenly change, their reflection dulling slightly. As my mind goes into overdrive once more, I feel the power in his grasp as he wraps an arm around my waist, taking me by total surprise.

"I'm going to do something right now, but I need you to trust me, okay?" he says, pressing his lips near my ear as he angles me closer to his body. Honestly, I really don't care what he says as long as he keeps me this tightly against him. Why is it such a turn-on to have a man with arms like his, strong and solid, pulling me tightly against him?

I'm doing everything in my power to not climb him like a tree, but we'll keep that to ourselves for right now, shall we?

I don't respond to his words, instead letting my body go limp, giving him silent permission to do whatever he needs. I'm relieved that I listened to my gut. It's as if the air has been pulled from the room as he slides his hands gently but decisively across my shoulders, his touch sending shivers down my spine. His fingers trail down my arms, brushing against my skin with a warmth that contrasts with the coolness of the room.

He cups my face with both hands, his thumbs lightly caressing my cheekbones, and tilts my head as his mouth slants across mine. The kiss is slow and deliberate, a tender dance of lips that deepens, a hunger there I hadn't anticipated. His touch is both electrifying and soothing, as if he's pulling me into a space where nothing else matters.

When he finally pulls away, I'm left reeling, my senses overwhelmed by the new rush of emotions. I'm so lost in this whirlwind of feeling that I don't immediately notice Amy standing in the doorway.

"Sorry," she says quietly, her voice barely above a whisper. "Just wanted to let you know I was leaving, Austin...er, Mr. Porter."

"All good, Amy," he mutters, his voice a little gravelly as he steps away from me. "Thanks and see you in the next few days?"

She looks at Austin, then to me, then back to Austin again. "No, my schedule changed recently, so I'll be coming in every Wednesday only from now on."

"Just one day a week, then?" Austin double-checks as she nods. There's a look on her face when she looks at him, though, that makes me realize what that kiss was for. He wasn't kissing me to kiss *me*, he was kissing me to get Amy to leave him alone. Or at least that's my best guesstimate.

Amy's gone a few moments later, leaving us alone with that kiss hanging in the air between us. As soon as I hear her car pulling away, I place a hand on my hip and point a finger.

"You did that on purpose."

The grin he serves me is a wicked one. "But it was fun, right?"

"Yes. No. Yes." I shake my arms in the air. "Argh! Not the point, Austin. You used me as a make-out red herring so Amy would think you have a girlfriend. Am I right?"

"Yes, but there's a reason," Austin explains, his expression sheepish. "She's got a crush and at first it was cute. Unassuming. I thought nothing of it, but she's gotten worse recently and has been really over the top with showing up when she's not scheduled. She brings me things, like dinner, when she's 'passing by' but come on. We live in the country. You don't just swing by when you're coming here."

He has a point. "Go on," I encourage him.

"She's only supposed to come one day a week, but she shows up at least twice a week. Does it under the guise of 'someone needs to check on you.'"

"You didn't think telling her the truth was better?"

He hangs his head. "Now I do."

I look around the room, at the now-finished bookcase. The smell of freshly dusted furniture and cedarwood fills the air. Looking back over at Austin, I find him staring at me with this sexy smile draped across his beautiful, full, bright red lips. Those lips were on mine mere moments ago and I want that warmth back.

I want to be irked that he used me to get Amy's attention, but when he's trying to ward off unwanted advances, how mad can I really be?

"You need to start drawing better boundaries, Austin." I point out the window in the direction of the lane. "You can begin by letting Amy know you aren't interested and then let her go."

"Are you wanting me to let her go because you're jealous?" He winks as he takes a step.

"No." I hold my hand out to stop him. "I think you need to nip it in the bud so no one is hurt."

"She's the one with the crush," he starts to whine, and I roll my eyes.

"Be the bigger person, okay?"

He takes another step. If I was to put my hand out now, my fingers would rest on his chest. His firm, tight, strong chest. The thought of letting my fingertips glide slowly across his bare chest sends a thrill through my system. I'm still in that daydream when he takes the last step, his body slamming into mine as he puts his arms around my waist again, and pulls me close.

"I don't know why you're doing this, Austin. It's not like I'm going to let you kiss me again," I whisper, not trusting my own words.

Hooded eyes meet mine, his hand slowly rising to cup the side of my face, then delicately stroking my cheek as his fingertips dance along my jawline. Shivers dance across my flesh and I fight back an audible groan.

"That's fine," he whispers, too. "How about I just do this?"

He leans in, his breath warm against my ear, sending a cascade of chills down my spine. His lips hover just above my skin, close enough to feel the heat of his breath, but not quite touching. He trails the ghost of a kiss along the curve of my neck, his mouth so close that every nerve in my body is on fire with anticipation.

His hand, still cradling my face, moves with agonizing slowness, the pad of his thumb brushing over my bottom lip, leaving me trembling under his touch. He's toying with me, pushing me to the edge without giving me what I want, what I need.

Until I can't stand it any longer—and that time is now.

Not even thinking—and not wanting to anymore, if I'm being honest—I let my hands fly up and land on top of his, stopping them cold. I slam my eyes into his as I put one hand on either side of his face and pull him closer.

He wants a kiss? I'll give him one he'll never forget.

THIRTEEN

Austin

I am not prepared. I am not ready, not one bit, when Bex suddenly steps closer. The look in her eyes shifts—soft but determined—and it's enough to make my heart skip a beat.

"Bex?" I barely manage to get her name out before she surprises me, taking my face in her hands, her touch gentle but firm.

"Shh," she murmurs, her breath warm against my lips. "You talk too much."

And then, her lips slant across mine, and she kisses me.

It's soft at first, just the lightest brush of her lips against mine, as if she's testing the waters. But then she leans in, and suddenly, it's not so gentle anymore. There's a sweetness in the way she kisses me, like she's savoring the moment, but there's also a hunger, a need that I didn't realize was burning in her. It's like she's been holding back for too long, and now she's done waiting.

My hands move to her waist, pulling her closer, but she's already ahead of me, pressing her body against mine as she deepens the kiss. There's something playful in the way she nips at my bottom lip, like she's teasing me, daring me to keep up with her. I'm more than willing to take that challenge.

Her fingers slide into my hair, and I feel a shiver run down my spine when she tugs just slightly. It's not rough, but it's enough to make my pulse race. She tilts her head, changing the angle, and suddenly the world narrows down to just this—just her. The kiss is everything at once: sweet and tender, hot and urgent, like she's pouring all her emotions into it, and I'm more than happy to catch every single one.

When she finally pulls back, I'm left breathless, staring at her like she's just knocked the wind out of me—which, in a way, she has. Her lips are slightly swollen, her cheeks flushed, and she's looking up at me with this mix of affection and mischief that has my heart doing somersaults.

"Wow," I manage to say, still trying to catch my breath.

She grins, that playful spark in her eyes. "I've been wanting to do that for a while."

"Yeah?" I can't help the grin that spreads across my face. "Can't say I'm complaining."

"Good," she says, leaning in to peck me on the lips one more time, this one softer but no less impactful. "Because I'm not done yet."

And just like that, she pulls me back in and I'm lost all over again, wondering how I ever got so damn lucky.

Her lips find mine again, and this time, I'm ready. I pull her closer, deepening the kiss as my heart hammers in my chest. There's nothing else in the world right now, just the two of us. I'm completely caught up in the feel of her, the way she fits against me like she was meant to be there all along.

But then, just as I'm getting lost in the moment, Bex suddenly pulls back, her breath coming in short, soft bursts. I blink, dazed and definitely not ready for this to be over.

She looks up at me, her eyes sparkling with a mischievous glint. "You know," she says, her voice teasing as she brushes a thumb over my cheek, "I usually get dinner first before the kissing happens."

I stare at her, momentarily thrown off by the unexpected joke. But then, I can't help it—a laugh bursts out of me, loud and genuine. "Is that so?" I manage to say between chuckles, still trying to process how she just flipped the script on me.

Bex grins, clearly pleased with herself. "Yep. But, I suppose I can make an exception this time." She winks, stepping back slightly, though she doesn't let go of my hand. "Though, now that I think about it, you do owe me a meal."

"Oh, I do, huh?" I'm still grinning like an idiot, my heart lighter than it's been in a long time.

"Absolutely," she replies, playfully poking me in the chest. "A girl's gotta eat, you know."

"Well, I can't have you starving, can I?" I say, pulling her back into my arms, unable to resist. "But just for the record, I'm pretty sure that kiss counts as the appetizer."

Her laughter rings out, and I swear it's the best sound I've ever heard. "Bold move, Austin," she says, giving me that look —a mix of affection and amusement. "But let's see if you can back up that confidence."

"Challenge accepted," I say, unable to keep the smile off my face. "But just so you know, dessert's on the house."

She raises an eyebrow, her lips quirking up at the corners. "Dessert, huh? You really are full of surprises."

"You have no idea," I murmur, leaning in for one more quick, soft kiss that leaves us both smiling like fools. "But first things first—"

Bex's eyebrows pop expectantly, but before I can say anything more, an alarm goes off in my pocket. Groaning, I reach in and pull out my cell phone. I'd set this reminder earlier so I wouldn't lose track of time.

I show it to Bex with a sheepish grin. "Sorry, but I've got something I need to go do."

She tilts her head, curiosity lighting up her eyes. "I thought you were a recluse?"

"So it's a bad thing that I have somewhere to go?"

She crosses her arms, teasing me with a smirk. "For someone who claims to only hang out at his house and maybe run an errand or two during the week, you sure do seem to disappear a lot. What secret life are you living?"

"Well, now you're just being nosy," I say with a wink.

"I live at the end of your lane." She steps back, straightening her shirt with a mock seriousness that makes me want to pull her in for another kiss. "Okay, well. That was unexpected."

"But nice," I quickly add, squeezing her hand. "We'd probably still be going at it if I didn't have to—"

"Yeah, yeah," she interrupts with a laugh, brushing me off as she grabs her keys. "I get the hint. You've got 'something' to do. I'll let you go do it and talk to you later?"

I'm about to nod when my alarm goes off again, more insistent this time, like it's mocking me.

Bex snickers, tossing a wave over her shoulder as she heads to the door. "Better get going before that thing starts yelling at you. And Austin?" She pauses, turning to give me a grin that sends my heart racing all over again. "Don't keep me waiting too long."

"I wouldn't dream of it," I call after her, watching her leave with a smile that I know won't be fading anytime soon.

As the door clicks shut, I take a deep breath, shaking my head at how quickly she's turned my world upside down.

But honestly? I wouldn't have it any other way.

FOURTEEN

Pex

Pages and Prose, Georgie's shop and Sweetkiss Creek's local bookstore, is a busy and popular spot when I stop in today. I love a delicious bookshop, but this one is special. Not just because it's tucked away in what used to be an old walk-up apartment in town that's now in the area's most vibrant shopping district. Nor is it because it's Georgie's store and she's my friend.

No, my affinity for this bookstore started last summer, before I moved here. I'd found out about Georgie's open mic nights. I think she called them *15 Minutes of Fame,* or something like that, and I don't know...it tickled something inside of me and I had to explore it.

Something I taught myself how to do is play guitar. I'm not great—I can only manage a few chords—but I did write a song or two. Nothing major, just something for myself. I had anonymity at that time, which also gave me the courage to jump up on that stage almost every night she hosted here.

Georgie sees me, giving me a quick wave as she finishes ringing up a customer. I wait another moment as she takes care of a few more folks who are waiting in line, watching as everyone clears out in about ten minutes. The bookshop is silent once again.

"Hey," she says, leaning across the counter like she's about to curl up on top of it and take a nap. "Wow. That was a rush. Not sure why we're so busy today, but I'm not going to complain. What are you doing here?"

I finger the pages of the latest bestseller she has on display at the counter. It's an ice hockey rom-com I've had my eye on, *Penalties and Proposals* by Anne Kemp. I grab it and slide it across to her and lean on the counter myself.

"Buying that," I say, "and also coming in for...girl talk?"

"Is that a question?"

"Pretty much. I think I want girl talk, but you may want to talk me out of a thing."

She tilts her head to one side. "A thing?"

"A thing I'm here to girl talk with you about."

"Is this like girl dinner?" she ponders.

That makes me scratch my head. "Not sure what you mean."

Georgie rolls her eyes playfully, swatting at the air. "Never mind. What's going on?"

"I may have kissed someone."

"You did? Don't leave me hanging...who?"

I stare at her and don't say a word. Within thirty seconds, her eyes almost bug out of her head as she stands up straight and stares into space.

"Oh. Oh!" She pushes a few strands of hair away from her face, grabs her stool, and slowly sits. "No. Austin?"

I only nod.

"Was it good?"

"Amazing."

"Good to know." She cocks her head to the side. "Is this a manipulation on your part because of that hedge?"

"What? No," I declare, standing back and pretending I'm

offended she'd even suggest it. "I hadn't thought of that, but it's a good idea. No, the kiss was great. Austin is complicated, but what happened after that confused me."

"What happened?"

"He just left."

"Left. Like left and didn't say anything?"

"No, he said, 'I've got to go,' and then left."

"So there was a goodbye."

"Yes. But, the kiss part was left dangling."

"Was it a first kiss?"

"It was a forced one." I fill Georgie in on what happened with Amy and she listens as only a good friend can.

"Okay," she says, clapping her hands together and rubbing them when I'm done. "So he used you to get Amy to back off." She eyes me and then simply shrugs. "C'est la vie."

"What? You're quite casual about where my lips have been."

"Your lips, sunshine, not mine. Seriously, Amy had it coming. I know her boss and she was going to remove her from Austin's job anyway. Apparently, she did the same thing to another single guy in town and it's getting tricky. She's a hazard, so just know that. That and the fact he is not interested in her."

"How do you know?"

"Did you walk in on him kissing *her*?"

She has a point. One I'll ignore for now because I'm here looking for evidence. "That's not my only issue, you know."

The sound of the bell from behind signals a new customer at the door. I turn around to find a pretty dark-haired woman standing with a huge grin on her face.

"Ets!" Georgie exclaims, waving her over to us. "Bex, this is Etta, or Ets as I like to call her. One of the first friends I made when I moved here. Etta, this is Bex. She knows Spencer and Amelia."

Etta smiles my way, a flicker of recognition in her eyes. "I've heard about you. You're Spencer's former assistant, you lived in California right?"

"I did," I say. "You know the Stolls?"

Etta nods. "I have a wine bar over at the campgrounds. Amelia helped me get on my feet and get that shop opened, and I'm glad I did. This past summer was amazing." She gives me the most genuine and warm smile I've seen in ages. "Welcome to Sweetkiss Creek, Bex."

"We're talking about boys," Georgie prompts her and Etta's eyes widen.

"Anyone I know?"

"Austin," Georgie whispers as Etta gasps like any new-to-me-girlfriend should. It's kind of amazing, the immediate bonding that can happen with women when we let our guards down.

"Ahhhh. My grumpy-pants McGillicuddy himself. How is old man crankerson these days?" Etta muses while Georgie shakes with laughter.

"He's got a new neighbor and he kissed her," Georgie says, nodding her head in my direction. I'm not sure I like this "let's talk about you like you're not right in front of us" scenario.

"Hello. I'm right here."

Etta stares at me. "Are you prepared for someone like Austin?"

My head tilts to the side on its own. "What do you mean?"

"The guy gets attention," Georgie pipes in. "There is a level of limelight and celebrity involved with a football player."

I hadn't thought about that. "True."

"But, saying that," Georgie continues, "you did work for Spencer."

Etta nods her head in agreement. "So you've been around people who are in the spotlight constantly."

"Yes, but it's different when you're dating the person

who's in the glare. They, in a way, have made peace with it. I'm not a big fan of it, that's why I've never dated anyone in the spotlight. I don't want it."

"Fair," Etta says as she puts her forearms on the counter and leans in. "I understand wanting to have your space."

Georgie eyes me knowingly. "It's the anxiety too, isn't it?"

Only Georgie would know that the other layer of me, the autoimmune layer, is one to worry about. Slowly, I nod.

"It's a choice like this that can add to my stress or maybe not. It all depends on how I deal with it, so I need to know I'm strong enough."

"Why do you need to be strong enough?" Etta asks, prompting Georgie and me to give her a quick education on my relationship with Graves' disease.

"So, I'd be making out with my neighbor, who is also my boss. There is so much wrong here. He's also super grumpy, and I know I'm rose-colored glasses sunshine sometimes. Too much close proximity and now we're also adding in too many rom-com tropes for my liking." I throw my hands in the air. "I'm overthinking this kiss. This one amazing kiss that made me go weak in the knees. Just because I want more doesn't mean he does, and I need to realize that not hearing from him for the last three days is a sign."

"He could have been getting ready for his return to his team, he may have had appointments." Georgie wags a finger my way. "You don't know. Have you spoken to him for work?"

I shake my head. "I've only emailed him since it happened. I wanted to give him space."

"So you haven't talked at all since his lips were—" She points to hers and makes a ridiculous kissy-pucker face that makes me laugh. "On your smackers?"

"No. But...space. You know?"

"Pfft," Georgie growls. "I'd be in his face, spraying my territory like a cat in heat. *Mine! Mine!*"

"Isn't that what a seagull says?" I muse as Georgie leans across the counter to swat me.

Etta, who has been silent this whole time, grabs her phone from her purse and starts tapping on it. "What I'm hearing, Bex, is that you have bad anxiety that can come with the Graves, too, right? Like the disease can make it worse?"

I nod.

"My friend, Dylan, has really bad anxiety." Etta taps away, then with a final touch, puts her phone down on the counter. "I know she has a list of things she uses to combat it."

I open my mouth to say thank you, but my own phone suddenly chimes. Speak of the devil. It's Austin.

I show Georgie who waves me to the back of the shop so I can take the call. Walking away, I press the phone to my ear.

"Hey." Austin's Southern drawl is like melted butter. Smooth. "Sorry to bother you, but I needed to touch base before I left town."

"Oh," I manage as my stomach dips. I can hear the intercom system for the airport in the background. "You're already at the airport?"

"Charlotte. It's a business trip that has come up suddenly, but I'm back tomorrow in the late afternoon."

"Got it." Of course. He's going out of town and he needs to get his assistant to help with something, doesn't he? And I am his assistant. "What do you need me to do?"

A noise from behind alerts me. Spinning around, I find both Georgie and Etta hunched over behind a bookshelf, pretending to be listening in. The pair's giggles turn into raucous laughter when they realize I've discovered them.

Fighting my own laughter, I put my back to them again and focus on Austin.

"We have unfinished business. I need you to be free. One night this week, for me."

"What?"

"I want to take you out, Bex." He pauses. "Will you go out with me to dinner this week?"

Behind me, two high-pitched squeals that could break glass sound off. Throwing the duo a look, I cover the phone with my hand, attempting to mitigate any auditory damage done. I also turn down the volume on the phone, so these two won't accidentally on purpose overhear anymore.

"I'd like that."

"Good," Austin says, his voice muffled as the voice on the speaker in the airport goes off again. A second later, he's back. "They've called my flight to board, so I'm going to go, but I'll be in touch as soon as I'm back. Have a good day, okay?"

We disconnect, and I close my eyes and giggle. I've got a date. A date with Austin. A date with a very handsome man who is also the best kisser I've ever let my lips come into contact with. Ever.

I don't even realize I'm holding my phone next to my heart until Etta starts laughing.

"Look, Georgie," she says between giggles. "She's doing the phone clutch."

Georgie tilts her head to the side and smiles. "Oh, bless. Yes, she is."

I look down at my phone. "The phone clutch?"

"Holding it close to your heart, like you're trying to keep him right here," Etta teases as she pats her own chest. "Trust me. We get it."

Her phone dings and she flips it up to read the text that has come through. "Okay, that's Dylan. She suggests you get a fidget ring and now. There's a jewelry store down the street that sells them. She highly recommends it for anyone who is anxious and also falling in love at the same time."

"What?" My head almost spins off its axis. "I didn't say anything about falling in love with..."

"You don't have to," Georgie interrupts as she waves a finger near my nose. "It's all over your face."

"No, no way I'm in love. Not yet."

"Keep telling yourself that, sweetheart." Georgie just smirks. "Take it from the both of us, the heart knows before the head does."

As she and Etta exchange a knowing look, I feel my pulse quicken. "You two are impossible."

Etta grins, leaning in. "And you're in deeper than you think."

I open my mouth to argue, but the words catch in my throat. Instead, I just shake my head, laughing nervously. "We'll see."

Georgie gives a playful shrug. "Oh, we already have."

FIFTEEN

Austin

The afternoon sun hung high over Tampa Bay, casting sharp shadows across the practice field. I lean against the cool glass of the box, eyes locked on the action below. My old teammates move like a well-oiled machine, each cut, each route as precise as I remember. The smell of fresh-cut grass mixed with sweat hit me, and for a moment, I let it take me back. This used to be home.

"You never thought you'd be back here, did you?" Coach Donovan's voice cuts through my thoughts, pulling me back to the present. His tone is gruff, but there is a warmth underneath it—one that has guided me through countless games.

I turn to look at him, catching the knowing look in his eyes. "Honestly? No."

Coach Donovan nods like he understands, like he always does. "But here you are. And you're moving like you've got something to prove."

"I do," I admit, though the words feel heavy. The excitement is there, bubbling just under the surface. The thought of putting on my pads again, feeling the adrenaline rush, hearing the crowd—it was what I'd fought for. But standing here at the stadium that made me a star, I'm starting to wonder.

"Austin." Coach leans in, his voice dropping low, serious. "You're ready. Your physiotherapist says you're ready. The team doctor says you're ready. I've never seen you in better shape. But if you're going to do this, you need to commit. Come back down here full-time, get into the rhythm with the team. We could have you on the field by the end of the month."

My heart speeds up at that. A month. That's all it would take. But even as I feel the rush, my mind is a thousand miles away, back in Sweetkiss Creek. Back with Bex. She's probably dealing with Mrs. Rosenblatt or another tenant right now, flashing the smile that turned my world upside down. The smile that lifts perfect pale-pink lips at the corners. Lips I finally got to kiss.

And that kiss. The kiss that opened my eyes even more to what a dolt I've been, sitting on the sidelines of my own world, going through the motions as I healed. The kiss that reminded me I can feel and I feel things pretty deep. The kiss that ignited a small spark.

A chance at...at what? A relationship? A good friendship? At love? The mere thought of love sends a thousand tiny goldfish swimming around my belly like they're in a sugar frenzy.

Love. Huh. That was something I never thought I'd have again.

"You'd have to come down as soon as possible," Coach presses, not seeing the battle going on in my head. "We need to see how you're doing, get you back into the playbook, shake off any rust."

I nod, but my thoughts are so far from this field I need a passport to catch up to them. This should've been an easy decision. I'd spent months dreaming about this moment, clawing my way back from injury, determined to prove everyone wrong. But now, when it's all within reach, the pull isn't as strong as it used to be.

Because back home, there is something—someone—I'm not ready to walk away from. The thought of leaving Bex, putting miles between us just when we are starting to find something real, makes my chest tighten. Which, considering it's been one kiss, sounds crazy but it's not. I've waited since I met her for her to be back in front of me. I added her to the list of people I started to push away when I thought I wasn't good enough anymore. Then, she gets delivered to my doorstep—well, next door, but close enough.

No matter what, it's something. It's fate.

"Think about it, Austin," Coach bellows, clapping a hand on my shoulder. "But don't take too long. We need to know where you stand."

Where do I stand? Right now, it feels like I'm stuck between two lives—one filled with the roar of the crowd and the thrill of the game, and the other with the quiet promise of something deeper, more lasting.

I'm just not sure which one I want more.

* * *

I'd gotten out of the meeting with enough time to get to the airport and run to my plane. It was good timing, really, because once I landed in Charlotte I had a few texts come in from Bex. She'd arranged for Mrs. Rosenblatt to get her new carpet today but, as the Gods of carpet-laying would have it, almost everything had gone wrong.

I scroll through texts updating me of the workmen's arrival with the wrong carpet, to their arrival with the right carpet, only to unroll it and find out they don't have enough. Then, apparently, there was a flat tire. It's all too much.

I don't bother getting in touch. Glancing at my watch, I

realize if I step on the gas, I'm close enough I know I can get to the building and go see Mrs. Rosenblatt myself and smooth things over.

It's almost five o'clock when I park my truck on the street outside of Mrs. Rosenblatt's. When I knock on the door, I'm as surprised to find Bex there on the other side as she is to see me.

"Hey," she says with a smile slowly creeping across her features. "Did you come straight here after you landed?"

I hold up my phone. "Seeing all these texts, you bet I did." I squeeze her arm and slide past, walking toward Mrs. Rosenblatt. She had been one of our first tenants and one that needed a little more hand-holding than the others, but she's always been nice to both me and to Levi.

"Austin, you didn't need to come," Mrs. Rosenblatt coos when she sees me. "Bex here has done her best today."

My eyes flick to Bex, who takes a small bow. "She's great. I bet she already has a new date on the books this week for your real carpet to be installed?"

"That's what we were just finalizing," Bex speaks up. She pulls out her phone, tapping a few buttons. "I included you on the calendar invite for this week. The guys will be back the day after tomorrow to install."

"They promised if they have any other issues, you get it free," Mrs. Rosenblatt says, wiggling her eyebrows.

"You like a bargain, don't you?" I tease.

"Oh, you know it." She holds up crossed fingers. "Here's hoping they forget something else. I'll get you a deal yet."

Cracking up, I turn and look at Bex, who is already putting her coat on. "We'll get out of your hair, Mrs. Rosenblatt."

"It was nice to see you, Austin," she says as she follows us to the door. "Thank you for having Bex here to help me today. She's been a delight."

My eyes lock with Bex's and, as if it has a magnet embedded inside it, my pinky slowly reaches out and takes hers, our fingers intertwined and linked in the most subtle of ways. Right here in the open, yet we're the only ones who know it's happening.

"Yes," I say without taking my eyes off Bex. "She is a surprise to me, too."

Bex blushes as Mrs. Rosenblatt pats my butt, making me jump in surprise. "Well, go on. You two get some rest, and you," she says, wagging a finger in Bex's direction, "I'll see you soon, yes?"

"You got it," Bex acknowledges with a giggle as the door closes behind us.

Leaving us, toe to toe, facing one another alone. Under the weight of her stare, my body begins to twitch on its own. Her hand rests on my forearm, and my skin, while protected from her touch between layers of clothing, still feels electrified, as if her touch was a torch and she was setting me on fire.

I drag my eyes to hers, a sensation deep inside of me beginning to fill my belly. Excitement. Anticipation. Want.

"How was your trip—" she begins to ask, but I go blank. I thread one of my arms around her, tucking my arm in the warmth that lies between her jacket and her sweater, clutching the fabric as I bring my mouth down, slanting it across hers. She tastes like hot chocolate and blueberry muffins, both signature recipes coming from Mrs. Rosenblatt.

The kiss starts slow, almost hesitant, as if we're both testing the waters. But then I deepen it, pulling her closer, feeling the warmth of her body against mine. Her lips are soft and sweet, and she melts into me, her hands gripping my jacket as if she's afraid to let go. My thumb grazes her cheek, tracing the curve of her jaw as I tilt her head slightly, allowing me to explore her mouth fully.

The world around us fades away; there's only her, her

taste, her warmth mingling with mine. It's intoxicating, a perfect blend of comfort and desire, and I never want it to end.

"What are we doing?" she asks as she pulls away suddenly, her tone hushed. She rests her head on my shoulder and sighs.

"I'm trying not to think about it," I respond honestly.

She pushes me away, gently but a push nonetheless. "I like thinking about it because I like thinking about you, but if we're not going anywhere, I need to know."

"You need to know now?" Lifting her chin with my thumb and forefinger, I place a soft kiss on the tip of her nose. "Why is that?"

"To guard my heart. Do I like being with you? I do." She stops talking as I place another soft, gentle kiss on her lips. "You challenge me in so many ways...but I'm scared. There's a lot that comes with dating someone like you."

"But, you've seen this before, right?"

Bex cocks her head and looks at me funny. "What do you mean?"

"Your former job, personal assistant. I'm sure you've dealt with some weird challenges."

"As an employee, yes. But not dating someone so public."

"You didn't date any celebrities?"

"No way!" She chokes on her laughter. "Y'all are high maintenance to work for, not even going to try to date one."

"But you said yes to a date with me."

She bites her lower lip, taunting me. "I did."

I stand up a little taller. "Guess I'm special, huh?"

"I can't get what I want from that hedge situation unless I win you over now, can I?" she says with a wink as she starts down the steps to the sidewalk and heads to her car.

There's no way I'm letting this woman go.

"Hold on," I call out, racing behind her. She is my guiding warmth at this very moment, she is the sun and I'm happy to be a planet in this woman's orbit. "Dinner. This week. What night are you free?"

She looks at me and shakes her head. "Why, Austin? Why me? Why have we gone from zero to one million in such a small amount of time? I'm not complaining because those kisses are white-hot amazing, but...why?"

"Because I spent months closing everyone out, including you. I remember seeing you at Georgie and Levi's wedding and I kicked myself in the butt because I couldn't get it together to come over and talk to you."

"What?" She looks at me with sadness flickering in her eyes. "Why?"

"I was hurt, not sure what the future held. I only knew football and the farm. You'd swept in, this cool girl from LA who might be moving here...and I started to feel something."

She waves a finger. "Wait. Remember you were dating someone named Stacey at that time. What about her?"

Ahh, Stacey. A social media influencer who showed up for her millions of followers, but couldn't be bothered to go to the hospital with the family when I was taken off the field on a stretcher. Self-serving, selfish, and self-involved.

"Funny thing, I was going to break up with her at that game in Charlotte." I wave my arms in the air. "When Georgie told me you were coming to that game, I'd made up my mind that I was going to ask you on a date. Then my life changed."

I watch Bex's face as the weight of what I'm sharing with her hits home. She snakes her hand out and wraps it around mine as she steps closer to me.

"Really?"

"Really," I say with a nod. "That's why I'm not going to take moments like this for granted anymore. I don't want to ignore the little things from now on. I wasn't seeing anything clearly until you came into focus, don't you get that?"

Bex grins, standing on her tiptoes and throwing both of her arms around my neck. "I do now."

"So, our date?"

"I can't do it tomorrow, but I can the day after."

"Friday it is," I say as I open the car door for her and watch her climb in. "How about I pick you up at six?"

"I'll be ready." She turns the key in the ignition and with a final wave, closes the door and pulls away from the curb.

Leaving me alone, standing under the most beautiful autumn sky coming to terms with the fact that I am, officially and unequivocally, falling in love with her.

SIXTEEN

The cool autumn air nips at my cheeks as we walk down the quiet street, the faint scent of wood smoke drifting on the breeze. Our first official dinner date was cozy, the kind where the conversation flows easily and the food is almost as good as the company. Austin had showed up right on time, looking effortlessly handsome, and picked me up with that easygoing smile that always makes me feel special. He even brought me a single white rose—simple, sweet, and unexpectedly romantic. So far, so good: the evening has been beyond what I would define as perfect. It's the kind of night that makes you want to hold on to every moment.

I pull my coat a little tighter, savoring the crispness of the evening, when my hand accidentally brushes against Austin's. The touch is brief, almost imperceptible, but it sends a little jolt through me.

Before I can pull away, his hand finds mine, warm and sure, his fingers threading through mine like it's the most natural thing in the world. My breath catches, and I glance his way, feeling a rush of something—excitement, maybe, or anticipation. It's such a simple gesture, but it feels like so much more.

His grip is firm but gentle, and I can't help the small smile that tugs at the corners of my lips. This thing between us, in this quiet moment, feels like we're finally starting to understand one another.

The evening is calm, with only the sound of our footsteps on the pavement and the occasional rustle of leaves in the wind. I'm acutely aware of his presence beside me, of the warmth of his hand and the way it makes everything else seem a little less cold, a little less uncertain.

I squeeze his hand, just a bit, testing the waters, and when he squeezes back, it's like a silent promise. We walk on, the world around us fading into the background, and for the first time in a long while, I'm content just to be here, next to him, our hands clasped together in the autumn chill.

Austin's gait slows as he indicates a park bench nearby. "Want to sit?"

"Sure," I say, following where he leads.

As we approach the bench, a couple walking past slows. The man sidesteps and plants himself in front of Austin.

"Austin Porter?" he inquires as Austin nods. "Thought so. I'm Thomas Landon, Tommy Landon's father."

A look of recognition floods Austin's features as he stands up and shakes Thomas's outstretched hand. "It's nice to meet you. Tommy is a good kid. He playing tonight?"

"Sure is, that's where we're headed now," he says, his eyes bright as he peers over Austin's shoulder to talk to me. "Sorry. He's been coaching my boy for months now and tonight he goes on the field for the first time. Ever."

"That's exciting," I say, making sure to give his wife, who stands nearby beaming as well, a quick wave.

"You guys headed over to watch the game?" she asks, her voice hopeful.

Austin looks my way. "Well, we hadn't planned on it..."

"But we can," I say, looking at Austin with my eyebrows raised in question.

"Well, hope we see you there," Thomas says as he grabs Austin's hand and pumps it once more. "And thank you for giving Tommy the self-assurance he needed to get out there again. We're forever grateful."

As they head off, I turn and look at Austin, who stands in front of me wearing a sheepish expression.

"If I'm not mistaken, that guy seems to think you've been helping his son out?"

Austin holds up a finger. "Okay. Give me a second, and I'll explain."

"First things first," I say, already getting the hint without him having to come out and say it. "Do you want to go to the game?"

He shrugs. "Yes, but I really want to spend time with you, too."

"You can do both," I say with a giggle.

He looks around, almost twitchy. I can sense something is up. "Did you have something you wanted to tell me?"

His eyes grow wide. "How did you know?"

"Ahh," I say as I rub my temples. "I'm woman. Me psychic."

Austin bursts into laughter. "Intuition?"

I point to his foot, which is tapping. "You're really fidgety all of a sudden. You can't hide anxiety from someone like me, remember? My energy feeds off of someone else's anxiety."

"Good point." He wraps his arm around me. "I was in Florida this week."

"You...what?"

"The other day when I had to leave town suddenly. I was in Tampa Bay. Coach Donovan wanted to see me in person to discuss getting into practice as soon as I can now that I've been cleared by all the doctors."

Every emotion inside of me twists. We're not together, so I can't expect anything, at least this is what I tell myself. Austin had his own life before I moved to the end of his lane, and now that life wants him back. I met him when he was playing football; I know how happy it makes him.

"So," I say, trying to keep the disappointment out of my tone, "you'd go back to Florida?"

He nods, slowly. "You know, if you really were a psychic, you would have seen this coming."

"Har, har," I say, smacking his chest. I want to turn my attitude about this around, because it's not about me. It's about him and what he's accomplished. This man didn't think he'd get on the field again. Ever. And now here he is, ready to play, and his old team wants him back. That's pretty exciting. "Well, congratulations, Austin. This is kind of a big deal, huh?"

"It is. I can't lie, I am really happy," he says, his arm tightening around my waist as he pulls me closer. "The whole time I've been recuperating, I wanted to have this happen. To be asked to come back to my team, to play more. I wasn't ready to retire. I'm not ready for that. Not now." He pulls away, one hand cupping the side of my face. "But I don't like the idea of not being here."

"Why is that?"

"Because I'm feeling like myself again. I want to show up for my family, I've got amends to make. And now there's you."

He kisses my forehead.

"Oh, stop it," I tease. "Now you're just being flirty."

"Nope, it's the truth. Now that there is a you and you are here, I don't like the idea of being in Florida as much as I'll need to be."

"Well, considering where we were when I first moved in

and how far you've come," I say with a wink, eliciting a chuckle from my reformed neighbor, "it won't be easy, but I know going to Tampa Bay may be the thing that makes you happiest. And I want you to be happy."

"Where does it leave us?" he asks.

"I don't know," I say as honestly as I can. "We're figuring things out, right? So we can't rush it."

He shakes his head. "I don't like it."

"What part don't you like? If it's the part about me, well, you need to get over that."

"I can't just 'get over that'—don't you get it? It's like you're a ball of light. A sunbeam I needed, and when you turned your illumination my way, I felt warm. For the first time in a very long time. Invincible. Like I can do anything."

"And you did," I exclaim, clapping my hands together and stepping away from him. Am I feigning happiness while Adele's "Someone Like You" plays on repeat in my mind? There's a song that's about to live rent-free for a few weeks. "Look at you. You're back, Austin Porter!"

"You make me better. You make me want to be better, so I am."

"I want you to feel that for yourself, and not just for me."

His head cocks to the side. "How do you mean?"

"I love the idea of making someone better, but it is a lot of pressure." I chuckle. "Although, diamonds are made under pressure, aren't they?"

"In sports, we say 'pressure is a privilege.'" Austin looks around, nodding his head as if he's made up his mind about something before he tugs on my arm. "Come on, there's something I want to show you."

* * *

The stadium lights blaze against the inky night sky, casting a golden glow over the football field below. The freshly painted white lines gleam, cutting through the deep green turf like crisp, precise markers of the battles yet to be fought. The air hums with energy, filled with the distant roar of the crowd and the rhythmic thud of drums from the marching band.

From our vantage point on a hill behind it, the field stretches out like a grand stage, the end zones promising victory or defeat, while the bleachers on either side are packed with cheering fans, their faces blurred but their excitement palpable. The smells of popcorn and autumn leaves mingle in the cool night air, completing the perfect picture of a Friday night high school game.

"Those are my guys," Austin murmurs, his eyes landing on the team as they huddle around a single man, who I assume is their coach.

"So this is one of those errands you've been running, huh? Yeah, you are such a recluse." I roll my eyes as his fingers dig into my side, tickling me. "Stop it!"

"I'll tickle more if you keep that up." He stands up a little taller as he watches them. "They helped me get out of my own way."

A silent understanding lands between us, settling into the comfortable space. Austin's eyes sparkle as they flit around the field, taking in the energy, the chaotic sounds, and the bright lights.

"Friday night, baby," I joke.

"It's nostalgic," he whispers. "They remind me of why I started. Their energy," he says as he waves a hand at the team, "got me back on track for performance. It was one aspect of my recovery I was obviously focusing on."

"What were the others?"

"Mindset and longevity. Longevity because I wanted to come back to the game, so I knew I needed to be persistent and also patient with myself. That's another reason this part was so important, working with the kids."

"And you didn't tell anyone?"

He shakes his head. "I told Levi when he needed to know."

"Mrs. Rosenblatt has seen you."

"She has?" His eyes widen with surprise.

I bob my head up and down. "Mentioned it to me, but I never asked."

"Why?"

"I figured if you wanted anyone to know what you were up to, you'd tell them." I nudge him with my elbow. "I'm not going to out your secret. No way, man."

"Thanks." He chuckles.

"And the mindset part?"

No sooner are the words out of my mouth before I hear someone scream Austin's name. Both of our heads spin as we look around and another voice joins the chorus. Then another. Within a few seconds, it becomes loudly obvious that the whole team has spotted us and is chanting for Austin to come to the field.

"Be right there!" he calls out, laughing as he turns to me. "You were asking about mindset? That"—he points to the teens—"has also helped. All for one and one for all. I've been a jerk, but I have been working on myself in the background. I pushed as many people away as I could, but I'm a lucky man because they all stayed by my side. They didn't give up even when I wanted to."

A feeling of warmth floods my veins. "That is a mindset all its own, isn't it?"

"To show up when you don't know what you're going to get? You bet it is. For me and those around me." He shakes his head. "But these boys reminded me to be resilient. They were losing last year, and this year, they're on the track to play in the state championships. Visualization, meditation, working out together. I was here with them as their coach instilled that routine and wow...I got to see them fly."

"Sounds like you did the mindset part of this to me," I say as he wraps his hand around mine and we start to walk down the hill.

"Yes, somewhat. But it's more than all of that." He stops short, whipping me into his chest as he wraps his arms around my waist. "You, Bex. You're fire. Your snappy comebacks, and the way you put me in my place. Those were the moments that I look at and can point to and say, 'I think I started to wake up then.' Because I was kind of on pause. I was going through the motions, but nothing had clicked. The day you showed up, my stakes got higher."

"Hopefully your standards, too?" I tease, resting my forehead against his.

"Definitely," he says as he smiles softly at my teasing, the warmth in his eyes making my heart flutter. Before I can say anything else, he closes the small space between us, his lips brushing against mine in a quick, tender kiss. It's brief but full of meaning—like a promise wrapped in softness. His lips are warm and inviting, and I can feel the sincerity behind them, like he's pouring all his unspoken feelings into this single fleeting moment. When he pulls back, his eyes lock onto mine, and I know without a doubt that something between us has just shifted, deepened.

He pulls back, his eyes still locked on mine, and without a word, takes my hand. There's something unspoken between us as he gently leads me toward the football field. The cool night air wraps around us, and the distant hum of the crowd and the sight of the field feels almost surreal.

We reach the edge of the field, and I let my gaze drift across the turf, the place where so many games have been won and lost, where so much emotion has been poured out under the bright lights. It's strange, really, how much this field means to him—and now, somehow, it means something to me, too.

As we walk along the sideline, hand in hand, I can't help but think about how falling in love feels like... well, like getting Graves' disease if I'm going to be honest.

It sneaks up on you when you least expect it, slowly taking over until you can't remember what it was like to be without it. It makes you feel things you never imagined, makes your heart race, makes you question everything—and yet, here I am, standing on the edge of something terrifying and beautiful, and I realize I'm completely okay with it, and no matter what, everything will be fine.

Austin squeezes my hand, and I glance over at him, his strong profile backlit by the blazing lights around us. This is one moment I wouldn't trade for anything. Because it's not just about falling in love with him—which I no doubt am beginning to—but it's about waking up, about finally feeling alive in a way I didn't know I was missing. The stakes are higher, just like he said, and even though that should scare me, it doesn't. Instead, it makes me want to dive in headfirst, consequences be damned.

I smile to myself, leaning into him as we continue to walk. If falling in love with Austin *is* a disease, then he's the only cure I want.

SEVENTEEN

Austin

The kitchen smells like fresh coffee and a hint of cinnamon, and the morning light filters through the curtains, giving everything a warm golden glow. I'm sitting at the old wooden table that's been in our family for as long as I can remember. It's covered in nicks and scratches, each one a reminder of the years we've spent around it—eating, laughing, arguing. Levi leans against a counter while our mother sits across from me, her reading glasses perched on her nose as she flips through the local newspaper.

"So, Tampa wants you back," Levi says, leaning forward with a skeptical look.

"It would appear that is the case," I reply, placing my mug gently back on the table. The warm coffee still lingers in my throat, a small comfort in this swirling mess of emotions.

Mom peeks over the top of her newspaper, her eyebrows arching in mild disbelief. "I'd think you'd be happier than you seem to be."

"I am happy," I say with a chuckle, leaning back in my chair. "I'm also conflicted."

Levi shakes his head, the incredulity clear on his face. "I'm home for a weekend, you ask me to come out to Mom's so we can talk, and you're going to tell me that after all the hard work you've put in to get back up to par—"

"And after putting us through so much at the same time," Mom interjects, her voice sharp with the reminder of my melodramatic and immature actions over the past eighteen months.

Levi wags a finger, the kind that's seen one too many family debates, at her. "Yes, to that, too. After all you've put us through, you're going to sit here and tell me that not only can you go back to the team you loved, but now you're conflicted about it?"

Does it sound crazy and absolutely absurd when he puts it like that? It does, and I'll be the first to admit it. It sounds like I don't appreciate what I have, like I'm somehow "better than" what's on my plate. But it's not about that.

I let my gaze sweep across the room, finally meeting Levi's with a resigned sigh. "Yes."

He looks at me as if I've just asked to borrow his last piece of pizza. "Yes?"

"To what you asked. Yes. I realize how insane it all sounds. My whole life has been off the rails since the day I signed with the Thunderbolts, really. It's like I've been on a roller coaster that won't slow down, and now, with this decision, it's like I'm trying to decide whether to stay on the ride or jump off and hope for a softer landing."

Mom sets the newspaper aside, her gaze softening. "Austin, sometimes life throws us curveballs and we have to figure out how to hit them. But just because something is difficult doesn't mean it isn't worth it."

Levi leans back, shaking his head with a mix of frustration and understanding. "Well, whatever you decide, just make sure it's what you really want. Because in the end, that's what matters most. Let's break it down. What's holding you back?"

I take a deep breath, searching for the right words. "It's not just about the football. It's about everything that comes with it—the pressure, the expectations, the constant grind."

As the words come out of my mouth, my mother grunts, shifting in her seat. I notice her pause, her brow furrowing slightly.

"Well, I think I know what the real reason could be," she says as she leans forward and tosses the open newspaper onto the table for our viewing pleasure.

She smooths out the paper on the table, right between us, and I see it—a photo of me at the game last night. But it's not just me. Bex is there, too, tucked against my side, her head resting on my shoulder. The way we're leaning into each other, it's obvious there's more going on than just watching a game.

Mom looks up at me, and I catch the glimmer in her eyes. She's got that look—part curiosity, part amusement, and a whole lot of knowing. "Well, would you look at that," she says, tapping the picture with a finger as she exchanges a look with Levi. "You and Bex made quite the impression last night."

I can feel my ears burn a little as I glance back at the photo. It's just a moment captured in time, but it feels like it's saying a lot more than I'd planned on. I lean back in my chair, trying to play it cool, but I can't help the small smile tugging at my lips. "Yeah," I say, my voice a little rough. "We did, didn't we?"

Levi pumps a fist in the air. "I knew hiring her to work for us would be the best idea ever."

"Shush," Mom yells, grabbing a stray piece of the real estate section, balling it up and tossing it Levi's way. "She's not a mail-order bride."

"True, but so you guys know, if it didn't work out I'd totally blame it on Georgie." He snickers.

"I'll let her know you said that," Mom grumbles as she

looks my way. "Ignore him. This is all making more sense now. What do you need from us, Austin?"

Goosebumps ripple across my skin as my mother's hand closes on top of mine. This family. Levi and I won the lottery when it came to moms; we got lucky. The fact she would ask how she can help me, yet again, after all the ick I've put them through is a testament to how amazing and strong this woman is.

Levi kicks a chair out and throws himself in it, sidling up to the table next to me. "I feel like I need a shot of whiskey for this conversation."

"You and me both," Mom mumbles as she grabs a diet soda out of the fridge, laughing. "Never thought Austin would be the one head over heels like this."

"Hey!" I wave a hand. "Hi. Still here. We can talk about Austin or we can talk *to* Austin. I know I prefer the latter."

Levi takes a can of diet soda from our mother and he turns so he is fully facing me. "So, go on, then. Tell us what you need."

"I've thought about this long and hard, and I don't want you guys to talk me out of it, okay? I need to do something that shakes things up for me."

I watch as their eyes meet, then they smirk at the same time as if they've practiced for ages to coordinate that tiny effort. Family.

Levi leans in closer. "I'm listening. I'm also available to help as needed."

"I'm liking the sound of this," Mom agrees, scooting her chair closer as well. "If it's about Bex, are we doing a grand gesture?"

"More along the lines of making a decision," I respond.

Mom's eyes soften with understanding. "Austin, you have to remember that life isn't always about choosing between one thing and another. Sometimes, it's about finding a balance that works for you. And sometimes, you can have both if you're willing to work for it."

Levi nods in agreement. "Mom's right. You've always been someone who dives headfirst into everything. Maybe this is just another opportunity to figure out how to blend what you love with what you need."

"And *that* is it." I nod slowly, feeling the weight of their support. "I guess I'm just afraid of making the wrong choice. What if I go back to Tampa and it's not what I hoped it would be? What if I'm not ready for that level of commitment again in football but I am ready to shift that energy in a different direction?"

Levi leans forward, his expression serious. "Listen, Austin. No decision comes with a guarantee. But you've worked hard to get to where you are, and you've got people who care about you and support you. Whatever you choose, just make sure it's a decision you can live with. And if things don't go as planned, remember that you've got the strength to adapt and overcome."

Mom reaches over and places a hand on mine, her touch warm and reassuring. "Follow what feels right for you, and don't be afraid to take a chance."

I look between them, feeling a surge of gratitude for their wisdom and support. "Thank you. This does help. It tells me that I need more than a favor."

Mom's eyes light up again. "We're back to the grand gesture?"

"Kind of," I say, my line of sight flicking to my brother. "However, what I think I need, and want, will require more than a grand gesture. It's going to need some serious magic."

"Woo hoo! I love it." Mom claps her hands as she reaches for her phone. "Where do we start?"

EIGHTEEN

Dex

Nothing beats the first sip of your pumpkin spice latte in the morning. There is something so welcoming and familiar about the flavor, it's like a warm hug for your mouth. Everything could be falling apart around me and I'd still be able to sit here and sip on this drink and enjoy every sip.

My fold-out chair isn't the most comfortable, but seeing as I decided when I woke up that today is the day I need to meet Jared, it's the one thing I could drag out to the mailboxes with me.

Today's theme song? Lou Reed's "I'm Waiting for the Man" works.

The sound of a breath of air being exhaled pulls my attention to my feet, where Harley sits. She'd spent the last few nights in the house, curled up at my feet. It's to the point now that my guilt is assuaged; the pet sitter knows if she isn't with her, she's here. Eventually, the owners will want her back, and I'll deal with that then, but for now I've got a dog.

In the distance, I can see a car making its way down the old country road toward our section of land. The car is red, bright fire engine red, so I know it isn't Jared. He drives a beat-up station wagon that doubles as the postal car. This car looks familiar, though.

Sitting back in my seat, I let my head hit the back of the chair as I stare up at the sky, thoughts of Austin tripping through my head: Austin going to Florida. Austin being on the road again. Austin back in football, which makes me happy, but that means—

A horn maniacally honking breaks my focus, taking my attention back to the car. The same red car that is now slowing down as it comes closer to my house, putting on its blinker. I wave, knowing with certainty it's Georgie behind the wheel.

"What are you doing sitting out here by the mailboxes on this beautiful sunny morning?" Georgie asks as she slams her car door shut and walks over to join me.

"Having coffee," I say, sweeping my arm around me as if this is a luxurious cafe where I await her company. "I'd offer you a chair but I didn't bring another one with me. Sorry."

"Please," she says, laughing. With her own flourish, she holds up her keys and taps a button on her key fob which opens the trunk of her car. She pulls out a folding chair of her own, closes the trunk, and joins me. "I am a woman who is always prepared...and who also went camping not long ago."

"I see," I say with a chuckle. My fingers are busy spinning my new fidget ring as she parks her butt beside me. "To what do I owe the pleasure of this surprise visit?"

Her line of sight goes to my hands and she smiles. "I'll have to tell Etta and Dylan you took their advice and got one of those."

"Yeah," I say, grinning at my hand, "I went and got it a few days ago. I've been feeling more settled, and better in general. This helps when I start feeling fidgety."

"Go figure," she giggles, reaching around my legs to scratch Harley's head. "So really. What are you doing out here?"

I look at her sheepishly. "I decided today was the day I wanted to meet Jared."

"As long as you're not stalking your neighbor," she says, patting my leg as she cranes her neck around, taking in the view. But she snaps her head back my way suddenly. "You aren't, are you? Stalking him?"

"What––," I say, choking on the most perfect sip of my latte. "No. I'm curious about Jared, that's all."

"The mailman who dresses up?"

I nod and toast the air with my mug. "I know. It's a good and busy life I have here in the country."

"Would there be another reason you're sitting out here?"

Is there? Of course there is. I hate admitting it to myself, and I'm going to hate saying it out loud to Georgie, too, but she's here and I'm feeling vulnerable.

But does that mean I have to tell her right now? I take another sip of my coffee and nod toward my house. "My HVAC is also getting fixed today."

"So being perfectly of right mind, you decided that was another reason to sit outside and hang out. You afraid he's going to drive by the place?"

Pursing my lips, I attempt to stare straight ahead, not wanting her to know she's got my number. But she does. I have a feeling if I didn't tell her how I was feeling, she'd already know anyway. I've discovered I have the kind of friendship with Georgie where it's like we've known each other for years. I'm grateful for it and know I'm super blessed she's my first real friend to have here in Sweetkiss.

Time to come clean.

"And I didn't want to sit in my house, looking across the field one more day wondering what's going on at"—I jerk my thumb over my shoulder—"his place."

"Ahh," she says, sitting back in her seat, her shoulders visibly relaxing. "Well, that's why I'm here."

"About me stalking Austin?"

"No," she moans. "Because Austin was called back to Tampa."

"Oh." Does my tone have an edge to it? Little bit.

"Do you want to talk about it?"

"Austin?" I'm playing a deflection game as she nods, and I shake my head.

A thousand words fly to my mouth at one time, but they're all caught at the exit, like a panicked crowd that can't get out of a stadium. I've been trying to figure out the feelings I've developed in such a short amount of time myself, but I can't. It makes no sense, until it does.

Because part of me knows that I began to fall for him the moment I met him, way back, before Georgie and Levi were married. I think in some ways my journey to Austin began the day she introduced us, and I just didn't know it.

"I'd rather not discuss the fact I'm falling for that man." I sit up a little taller, refusing to get teary.

"Okay," Georgie says, putting her leg underneath her as she angles herself on the chair, pulling sunglasses off their perch on her head so they rest on her nose. "Then we'll just sit here and not talk about Austin."

"Great," I mumble as my phone rings in my lap. Recognizing the number in a blurry kind of way, I answer. As soon as I hear the voice, I know it's Harley's pet sitter.

"Is she with you?" Felicity asks.

I look down at the dog sleeping peacefully at my feet. "Sure is. I guess you guys will need to get her back for the owners?"

"Well, that's the thing." She half-laughs. "I'm calling you with a weird question. Like, so weird I've never done this before." She's quiet for a moment before pressing on. "The owners have been back for a few days now, actually."

That's surprising. "Really?"

"Yeah. They told me not to contact you, they were going to. But then this morning they called and wanted me to ask if, well—would you like Harley?"

"Yes!" The word leaps from my mouth before I have a chance to digest what she's saying. But of course I would. I do. Why wouldn't I? "It's a little obvious that we're kind of made for each other, I think."

"Right?" Felicity cackles on the other end. There is something about this woman that makes me think she and I could also be good friends. Or at least, I know a great pet sitter now who lives in the area. "That was my thought, but it's still weird that they asked. They said since they're moving, they're worried it may not be best for her. Turns out she's not been very warm and connected with them as a family. She sleeps outside when she's with them and doesn't like being around anyone at their house."

All I can think about is how Harley likes to follow me from room to room, and even outside, like we're attached. I've seen her do it with Austin as well. "That's the exact opposite of when she's here."

"That's what I told them. I think that helped them make the decision because it's what's best for Harley, you know?" There's a rustling noise on her end of the phone, sounding like she's moving. Probably busy walking dogs. "I'll let them know I spoke to you. They'll want to drop her things off to you, meet you and all that, if that's okay?"

Shocked, but delighted, I agree to anything they need and hang up, jaw slack as I look at Georgie. "Looks like I've got a dog."

She lets out a low whistle. "You're a very busy lady out here at your mailboxes, aren't you?"

"Who knew?" I say as I toss the phone in the dirt by my feet. When I look back up, my wait is finally being rewarded: I see an old beat-up station wagon barreling down the old road, going at least eighty miles an hour, making a beeline for our place.

Jared.

Gripping my mug, I look over at Georgie. "I cannot wait to see what he's wearing today."

"I hope it's good. Like a lion costume or maybe a koala bear."

You can't wipe the smirk off my face as the wagon slows down, turns on its blinker, and pulls into the lane. Said smirk does begin to fall though once Jared exits the vehicle, cocking his head to one side and giving both Georgie and me a look like we're aliens he's found in the desert.

Turns out today isn't a day that Jared is dressed up. Today is the day we get to meet normal Jared, not dressed up and not wearing any makeup Jared, who looks like he's about twenty-nine years old, with blond hair that's been bleached from too much time in the sun and a perfect set of teeth that he shows off with a giant, welcoming grin. While I'm slightly disappointed there is no strange dress-up vibe today, I'm now intrigued. More so than I was even yesterday.

"Hi?" he says, almost in a questioning manner. Guess it's not every day you pull up to the mailboxes on your route and find a couple of women sitting and having coffee. "Are y'all like the welcoming committee?"

Out of the side of my eye, I can see Georgie's mouth hanging open. Being the good friend I am, I lean over and gently close it using the tip of my pointer finger. I turn my attention back to Jared, who holds out a newspaper and a stack of mail for me.

"Nope, just enjoying the day," I lie through my teeth.

"Okay." He looks at Georgie, then back to me. "I guess... have a good day?"

"You guess right," Georgie purrs as I kick her foot. Subtly

is not my thing. When I see she's still staring, I toss the newspaper at her.

His face twists as he gives us one last look over his shoulder before he hops back behind the wheel of his car, throws it in reverse, and takes off, leaving us in a trail of dust as he blazes away.

"So, Jared is cute," Georgie says, cracking up. "Wow!"

"You're too much," I manage between giggles. "Please tell me you know someone single to set him up with?"

"I'll find someone." She laughs, bending over to swipe the newspaper, but she pauses. She looks over to me and points. "Did you see this?"

The headline screams *"Local football star headed back to Tampa Bay?"* and has two photos accompanying it: one of Austin, looking devilishly handsome, and the other from the day he was taken off the field in Charlotte on a stretcher.

I don't have to hold the paper to get the gist. I know the gist. I'm living the gist.

I shrug. "That's why I don't want to talk about it."

Georgie tosses the paper to the side and turns her chair so we're facing one another. "You know, just because he'd be in Florida during training doesn't mean you can't have a relationship, right? People do long distance all the time these days. I know someone who made long distance work with a guy in New Zealand. They're married now."

"Sounds like an urban myth."

"Pfft. I'll get you her number. You can talk to her yourself."

I shake my head. "I've got no time for miracles."

"Yet you were just given a dog out of thin air."

I roll my eyes. "Not the same thing."

"Then what? Explain it to me. Why him? Why do you like him?"

Oh boy. Things I've been asking myself since I saw Austin last. Why *is* it him?

"I shouldn't feel anything for him, that's for certain. He's kind of my boss, he lives literally next door, and he's been off and on rude to me since I arrived. I want to remove a hedge that sits on our property line, one that he doesn't want me to touch, which kind of makes him my nemesis. Yet, when I'm in the same room with him or anywhere near him, all I can think about is him. It's like the air is pulled from me and I'm in a vacuum that exists for him."

"And he's such a ray of sunshine—" Georgie starts to say, but I hold up a hand to stop her.

"He is, actually, it's just everyone around him forgot." I turn so I can face her. "Nobody's fault, it's just a pattern that was easy to slip into for everyone. Including Austin."

"And you see something different?"

"I do," I say as I nod. "He was so interesting to me when I met him because he was so good. I fell for him then and held a torch for him until I moved here. Then, I see him again and he's changed. Yet at the core of it all, he is still Austin, right? I wanted to give him a chance because good people mess up. Good people make mistakes. Good people stumble."

"But you weren't seeing all the good when you first got here," she says with her voice low. "Yet you stuck it out."

"Well, I could see the potential. The greatness," I say, wagging a finger in the air. "Great people get back up. Great people don't see themselves as falling to the ground, they see it eroding up to greet them. Great people give reality a good PR spin because they get it. It's about what is in"—I tap my head —"here. And he's got a lot going on up there, let me tell you. And it is sexy."

For the second time this morning, I watch as her mouth goes slack. Again, being the good friend I am, I lean over to close it for her.

"Thanks," she whispers.

The sound of yet another car pulling into the lane makes us turn our heads. It's a dark blue van with "Anderson's Cleaning" painted on the side. Sitting in the car are two older women, I'll guess about fifty or so, waving to us as they scoot past, headed for Austin's.

I look at Georgie and shrug. "Not sure who they are."

"That's easy," she says with a wave of her hand. "The new housekeeping service."

Our eyes meet, and we can't hold our laughter back any longer. We take each other's hands and crack up, the sound echoing across the fields, filling the air with our joy.

"So, now what?" Georgie asks as the laughter dies down and we settle back into our seats.

I look out across the fields, feeling the warmth of the moment still lingering. "I'm not sure," I reply, my voice soft but sure. "For once, I don't have all the answers, and maybe that's okay. Maybe it's exactly what I need."

The uncertainty no longer feels like something to fear—it feels like the beginning of something new, something that could be even better than what I've imagined.

But only time will tell.

NINETEEN

Austin

"So, it's officially official," Emma announces, handing me a manila folder and giving my back a solid pat. "You're cleared to return to the field. Healthy as a horse."

"Yeah?" I ask, not wanting to move for fear that something, anything, could happen now to burst my happy bubble.

Emma nods. "Yeah. Go ahead. Be happy, you did it."

"Yes, I did!" I pump my fist in the air like I just won the Super Bowl and scoop her into a bear hug. "Thank you. Seriously, thank you for everything."

"You did all the heavy lifting," she says, laughing as I drop her back in place. She bends down to pick up her pack, slinging it over her shoulder like she's headed off to the next adventure. "I showed up, barked orders, and made you sweat."

"You also dealt with me, my overly involved family—"

"And your housekeeper," she interrupts, raising an eyebrow. "Who the rumor mill has said, by the way, got canned."

"Wasn't me," I say, holding up my hands like I'm under interrogation. "I was actually going to file a complaint this week."

"Well, word around town is she took it too far with some new billionaire who's slumming it on a houseboat. Apparently, he caught her lying on his bed, wearing a baseball hat of his, and probably sniffing his pillows."

"She was sniffing his pillows?" I say, my eyes threatening to bug out of their sockets.

"I said probably, not that it was certain," Emma says, wagging a finger my way. "This is how gossip begins."

"You started it." I shake my head, trying not to laugh. "But, to be fair, we knew she was going to get herself into trouble."

"Apparently, her mom works for the local police department." Emma chuckles, a mischievous glint in her eye. "Twenty bucks says she ends up in the county jail, courtesy of her mom. Tough love, small-town style."

"You could only get away with that in Sweetkiss Creek," I agree, biting back my own laughter.

"Anyway," Emma says as she taps the folder in her hand, drawing my attention back. "I spoke to Coach Donovan for you. Anyone else need a nudge?"

I grab a scrap of paper, scribbling a number on it, and hand it to her. "Yeah, give this number a call. Let them know I'm cleared for practice. You'd be saving me a lot of hassle."

"Will do." Emma's attention shifts as a rustling sound comes from the archway leading into the living room. We both look and find my new housekeepers, both in their early sixties and rocking silver hairstyles that my mother calls "chic," chatting away to one another as they shuffle by.

"The new order?" she queries, one eyebrow arched.

"You bet it is. They're both too busy with their own families to even think of making an extra casserole each week for little old me."

Emma snickers. "Have you checked your sock and underwear inventory?"

"Not yet, but I will. I think I need to keep an eye on the shorter one of the two. She seems shifty."

Emma laughs. "She's untrustworthy?"

"I've only deemed her to be sus," I say, making her laugh again.

We head toward the front door, and as I open it wide, my eyes drift to the house at the front of the property.

"So," Emma says, noticing where I've focused my gaze. "How are you feeling about heading to Florida these days?"

"I'll feel even better," I say, tapping the paper in her hand, "once you make that call. Text me when it's done, okay?"

She gives me an odd look but laughs it off as she heads down the steps. "You got it."

I watch her car disappear down the driveway before finally shutting the door. Emma's been by my side for the last eighteen months, pushing me to get back on my feet, and now here I am—ready to tackle life again.

And it feels pretty darn amazing.

Pulling out my phone, I dive into the next phase of my plan. Tomorrow night isn't just another Friday—it's the culmination of months of rehab, determination, and more than a few sleepless nights. It's my chance to finally take back control, both on the field and off. It's a goodbye to what was and hello to what will be.

I've been dreaming about this moment, and now that it's within reach, there's no way I'm leaving anything to chance. Everything has to be perfect, starting with Bex. I look out the window, staring at her house with such intensity that, for a moment, I swear my gaze could set the field ablaze. Dragging my eyes to the hedge that seems to sit between us, literally and figuratively, I can only imagine her delight if I managed to set *that* on fire.

Bex. The thought of her makes me smile. It's amazing how when you meet someone, and not just anyone, but your someone, things change. Doors seem to open that didn't before, and you have ideas that pop into your mind—call it divine inspiration? I don't know—whatever it is, it's the essence of what falling in love means to me.

When I was young, falling in love meant big feelings. Drama. It was embellishment, not sacrifice. But if you were sacrificing, you couldn't do it at your own chagrin. Yet, since Bex has come along, I'm realizing that I don't like that definition. I'm not a fan of what I once thought. I want more.

I want a better half, but I want to be here to lift them up, too. I want to show up and be my best so I can light us up, not wait for her to shine her brightness to keep us afloat, nor should she have to worry about me either. I like the independence, and the intertwined. The balance of it all. The sunny side to keep things bright and light.

I want Bex.

She's been on my mind constantly, and tomorrow night is my shot to show her how much she means to me. This isn't just a game; it's a play for something real, something lasting. I need to get it right, down to the smallest detail. I want her to look back on this night and to know I moved mountains for her, and only for her.

I can already picture her now with the lights of the field catching in her eyes, the noise of the crowd fading into the background as she looks at me. It's a moment I've been building toward, and I won't let it slip through my fingers.

I fire off a quick text:

> You and me, this Friday night, at the Sweetkiss Creek High School football game. Sound good?

Her reply is almost instant.

> Sounds great! How should I dress?

Casual, but it's homecoming, so, you know, maybe a little special.

Awww. I never went to my own homecoming...so this will be perfect.

I pause, her words giving me an idea.

I'm helping coach on the sidelines for this last game before I head out. I'd love for you to be there.

I wouldn't want to be anywhere else. xo

Her response makes me grin so wide, it feels like my face might split in two.

Everything's coming together.

TWENTY

Dex

The night sky is a deep indigo, dotted with stars that peek through the thin veil of clouds, casting a soft glow over the Sweetkiss Creek High School football field. The bright stadium lights flood the field, cutting through the cool autumn air and illuminating a sea of fans.

As I throw my car into park, I stop and take a moment to scan the lot. Austin had said he'd meet me here, but when he called to tell me this, I was a bit out of it since I was waking up from a nap in my nice and warm home, thanks to my fixed heating unit, snuggled with my new dog on the floor.

Don't judge me because I went out and bought one of those dog beds big enough for me and Harley. Just don't.

Swarms of people mill about the parking lot, and even more stand in groups dotting the hillside around the high school stadium on this special night. A huge banner erected over the field in colors of red and black, what must be the school colors, announces it's "Sweetkiss Creek High School Homecoming." Somewhere nearby the school marching band plays and the smell of sugar and fried food assaults my senses and reminds me of being on the main course of a carnival.

As I step out of my car and hear the familiar roar of the crowd in the distance, I can't help but feel a thrill of anticipation. Even though I've been to many football games in my time, I'd never made it to a homecoming game. It's not that I wasn't into it, I just wasn't into the dance and all of the other traditions around the whole pomp and circumstance of it all. So, I'd never bothered with the game at that time of year. Why go if I wasn't going to the dance, too, right?

As I walk toward the entrance, the irony that I spot Mrs. Rosenblatt making her way down the path with another older woman doesn't pass me by. With a cheeky grin, I make my way over to her, and Mrs. Rosenblatt waves enthusiastically in my direction. I wave back, squinting to see who she's with.

"Evening, Bex!" Mrs. Rosenblatt calls out, her voice carrying over the crowd.

"Hi, Mrs. Rosenblatt! How are you?" I ask as I navigate the throng over to the pair. "Out supporting the team for homecoming?"

"It's our alma mater, you bet we are," she says as she gestures to the familiar woman beside her. "Bex, you know Pearl, right? She's also a tenant of the Porter boys. The one who had that little...incident with the fire in her kitchen a few months back."

"I do." Pearl gives me a sheepish smile, and I return it, nodding in recognition. "Nice to see you again, Pearl. Thanks again for that beautiful bouquet of flowers. I'm glad everything turned out okay after the excitement."

Pearl chuckles softly. "Oh, just a little kitchen mishap."

"Something about the two of you," I say, grinning. "Between fires in kitchens and the smell of sangria in your bathroom, I sometimes wonder if you're running a speakeasy out of the Porter brothers' apartments."

Mrs. Rosenblatt gasps dramatically as she gives me a

conspiratorial wink. "Now, Bex, that's a secret we might just have to keep, isn't it?"

The thought of these two running a black market for booze and good times almost makes me spit with laughter. It's a visual I'll never get rid of. "Well, if you are, I hope you're getting good business."

"Never a dull moment, that's for sure," Pearl adds with a twinkle in her eye.

"I saw Austin down at the field earlier," Mrs. Rosenblatt says. "So it was him I've been seeing here all those times?"

I nod. "He's lending a hand and coaching from the sidelines tonight."

"Even more exciting," she says as Pearl bobs her head in agreement. "We both saw him play when he was growing up. It's exciting to have been on the proverbial sidelines ourselves and watched his career, and to see where he is now."

"Oh, I know!" Pearl exclaims. "It's wonderful, isn't it? From being a little guy who got into everything to being one of the high school superstars."

"More than that." Mrs. Rosenblatt rolls her eyes and shakes a finger at her friend. "You know he and Levi bought those buildings, like the one we're in, so that the rents wouldn't go up any more?"

I didn't even know that. "What?"

"Yes," she says, turning my way. "He never told you?"

I give a shake of my head, wondering what else that mystery man of mine is up to. When the mysteries are this sweet, you can bet I don't mind them.

"I had no idea, but knowing him and his brother, I can see that being a very good reason for them to get into real estate."

"Their mother taught them well," Pearl says as she holds her wallet in the air. "Now, excuse us, young lady, but I need a beer. Are you ready?"

I'm trying my hardest not to laugh as this dynamic duo

trots off in the direction of the concession stand, after a beer that I'm not sure they'll find at a high school football game but what do I know? Wrapping my coat tighter around my body, I continue toward the field.

Near the entrance, the sound of the marching band fills the air again and I walk through the gates. The stands are already almost full, with small groups of people hanging around in clusters around them. There's a hum of excitement that's impossible to ignore.

I glance around, searching for Austin, but still don't see him anywhere. My heart gives a little jump when I think about how much this game must mean to him. It's the last one before he heads off to Florida, and I know it's bittersweet for him.

Someone pushes past me, so I move closer to the field, standing by the gates where the players will come out. The anticipation builds as the crowd quiets down, all eyes on the tunnel where the team is about to emerge. Suddenly, the first few notes of "I Hope You Change Your Mind" by The Chainsmokers start playing through the speakers, and I can't help but smile. The song seems fitting, somehow, like the universe is playing DJ to our lives.

As the music plays, I glance around the stands, taking in the scene. My eyes catch on a familiar group in the crowd. His mom beams with pride, her smile a mirror image of Austin's. Next to her, Levi and Georgie chat away, both wearing Sweetkiss Creek sweatshirts to show their school pride. Of course they're all here, showing their support. That's what the Porters do.

When they notice me looking, they wave enthusiastically, and I wave back, feeling a warmth spread through my chest. I can't help but feel like I've gained some traction here, in my new town. This is truly shown in the evidence of me being at a local high school football game and knowing people in the crowd, though, isn't it?

Still grinning, I turn my gaze back to the field, my thoughts shifting to Austin as the team comes bursting out of the tunnel, the players starting to sprint onto the field with all the energy and enthusiasm of high school athletes who have nothing to lose. As I look around one last time, my eyes finally land on Austin, tall and confident as he stands by the bench, huddled with another man, hands waving, probably talking strategy. His eyes slam into mine as he waves, and I wave back, feeling a flutter in my chest.

The noise and cheers around me bring me back to the tunnel and the players. These guys are bursting onto the field ready to seal the deal and win a game. Part of me feels a little bad for the opposing team; even I can feel the palpable energy the home team is bringing today.

But then something unexpected happens. One of the players suddenly deviates from his course and runs over to me, thrusting his hand out.

"Here."

I look at the small bunch of greenery in his outstretched hand. "Huh?"

"It's for you," he says. He shoves it my way again. "Here."

Slowly, I reach out and take the bunch of shrubbery out of the kid's hands. Inspecting it, I turn it over and look at it, but am admittedly confused. Figuring it's a weird fluke, or a dare, I sit back and watch as the next player comes charging out of the tunnel. He does, and as he's about to run over to the bench he, too, does a pivot and jogs to me, extending his arm to give me something.

"M'lady," he says, giving me a deep bow and holding out another bunch of greenery.

"What is this for?" I ask him as I take the gift.

He shrugs. "I just do as I'm told." And with a quick salute, he's off, jogging over to the bench. I watch as he makes his way, my eyes connecting with Austin's. When I hold up the two small bunches of greens, he throws his hands in the air.

"Excuse me," someone says. I turn my attention back to find another football player standing in front of me with the sweetest smile on his face. "Sorry to bug you, but I was told you'd enjoy this present." He then whips out his own tiny bundle of greens. This time, as the player runs off, I bunch my bundles together and look at the leaves. If my eyes don't deceive me...

It's boxwood.

And so this continues. Each player, as they pass by, makes a sharp ninety-degree turn to their left and heads in my direction to hand me a small bunch of boxwood. My mouth falls open in surprise each time, and I can't help the laugh that bubbles up as the pile grows bigger and bigger. Pretty soon, a giant cooler bag is donated to me to carry them all, thanks to a kind high school boosters family sitting nearby and witnessing the whole thing.

By the time the entire team has passed, I'm the keeper of enough pieces of boxwood that I could build my own hedge right here if I wanted.

"What are you doing?" I finally manage to ask, calling out over the hubbub around us and staring at Austin incredulously as he jogs over to me, a grin spreading across his face. "What am I supposed to do with this now?"

"Maybe we can move the hedge somewhere else?" Austin's smile widens as he reaches out and pulls me into his arms. His hands wrap around my middle as he tugs on my waist and pulls me closer to him. "Or we could cut a window in it, so you have that view you want."

"That was my thought, too." I giggle, standing on my tiptoes to kiss his cheek. "But seriously, this is a lot of boxwood. When did you get time to clip all of this?"

"When you were sleeping," he says, tilting his head to one side as he looks at me. "I watched you with my binoculars one night until you went to bed, then..."

I slap his chest. "Stop it."

He throws his head back and laughs. "Well, know that I did it when you weren't around, okay?"

We stay here for a moment like this. It's as if the world around us has stopped moving and we're the only ones here. Surrounded by chaos and energy and noise levels like no other, yet it's all fallen away and there's a bubble. In that bubble is me. And beside me, with his arms wrapped around me is Austin. Our bubble.

Austin shifts his weight, his eyes hooded as he pushes a few stray pieces of hair out of my face.

"I wanted you to know I'm all in with you, Bex," he says, his voice low and serious.

"Really?" I ask, searching his eyes for any hint of hesitation. "So you think we can do this, even with you in Florida?"

"I do," he replies, his grin turning mischievous. "If I was going to Florida."

"What do you mean, 'if'?" I ask, my heart skipping a beat.

"As of this afternoon," Austin says, his eyes sparkling, "I've been signed to the Charlotte Cardinals. I'll be closer. A lot closer."

He then steps away and nods toward where his family sits in the crowd. As I follow his gaze, I look up to see that Mary, Levi, and Georgie are all wearing Charlotte Cardinals jerseys now and cheering. When I look closer, Georgie is waving one in the air.

"What is Georgie doing?" I ask. "And weren't they in Sweetkiss Creek High School garb a second ago?"

"She's holding your jersey." Austin shakes his head with embarrassment, a pink flush hitting his cheeks. "They all thought it would be funny to come wearing other clothes and then change for the big reveal. They've been more excited about this than I am."

"About what?" My head spins back and forth between Austin and his family as I blink at him, trying to process what he's just said. "Wait. You're not going to Florida? You're staying here?"

"I sure am," he says, brushing that stray piece of hair that won't stay put behind my ear. "As of this afternoon, I'm officially playing for the Cardinals. A certain coach"—he points to Levi—"helped to let the right people know I was back, but that I wasn't interested in going far."

"Okay." I want to understand, but it's a lot coming at me at once. Operation overwhelm is in progress. Austin threads his fingers through mine as I drag my eyes to meet his. "What does all this mean?"

"I want to be near you, Bex. I'm done being—what did you call me? 'Mister Grumpy pants'? I want to make this work."

"You're not just doing it so I lay off about the hedge, are you?" I tease, pointing to the cooler bag stuffed with pieces of boxwood.

"No way," he responds. "I want you to spar with me and to always hold me to task, show me new ways to see things and offer your perspective. I fully intend for us to come back and talk more about that stinking hedge. But we can table that discussion for now, as you put it."

For a moment, I'm speechless. All I can do is stare at him, feeling the warmth of his surprise as it wraps me in a delightful hug. This man. I feel like we've gone from one length of the football field to the other and then back again, the whole time navigating our way through barbed wire. Yet we're here. Together.

He's the one for me. I've known it since the day we met,

and about time. He's *finally* caught up. Which is fine, boys do mature slower than us ladies, don't they?

Without thinking, I lean in and kiss him, pouring all my feelings into that one moment. The crowd around us cheers, but it's like we're in our own little world, just me and Austin and the promise of what's to come. And it's a good one.

When we finally pull apart, I'm breathless, my heart pounding in my chest worse than a Graves palpitation, but that's okay by me. "You're really staying," I whisper, almost afraid to believe it.

"I'm really staying," he confirms, his forehead resting against mine. "And I'm really in love with you, Bex. I want this. I want us."

There's a feeling of wetness on my cheek, tears I didn't know were going to spill take this time to do so. "I'm in love with you, too, Austin," I say, my voice shaking with emotion. "And I want this more than anything."

He kisses me again, and I know, most certainly and without a doubt, that this is the start of something amazing. Something perfect. A story we'll tell our grandkids one day—if they're lucky, that is.

It might not be a perfect fairytale ending, but it's ours, and that's more than enough.

TWENTY-ONE

Epilogue: One Year Later

Bex

The crisp autumn air bites at my cheeks as I settle into my seat, surrounded by the roar of the stadium. It's the perfect fall day in Charlotte, and with the scent of buttery popcorn and hot dogs drifting on the cool breeze, mixing with the sharp scent of fresh-cut grass from the field below, it smells like football. My heart starts beating a little faster, the energy seeping into my pores. The crowd is electric––it's hard to not get swept up in the excitement with a sea of fans all dressed in team colors stretching out around me, buzzing with anticipation.

From up here, the players look like warriors, moving in perfect formation as they take their place on the field. But my eyes are fixed on one warrior in particular—MY warrior. Austin. He's out there in his jersey, helmet glinting under the bright stadium lights, and man does he look good. My heart races in time with the rising noise of the crowd. I can't help but feel a surge of pride and excitement, watching him move with the grace and power that only someone with his talent has. It's so good to see him back in his element.

The trees just beyond the stadium have turned to brilliant shades of red, orange, and gold, framing the field in autumn's vibrant palette. The setting sun casts a golden glow across everything, making the moment feel like we're in a film. I pull my jacket tighter around me as the temperature dips, the evening settling in.

"So much fun to come to these games now, right?" Georgie asks, nudging me with the pointy tip of her elbow. She turns around, no doubt looking for Levi who'd been pulled into a VIP suite as we made our way past.

"It really is," I smile as I grip her knee. "It's been so good to see him perk up again. Austin's been on cloud nine since he made the decision to stay closer to home."

"He made the decision to stay closer to Bex," Georgie grunts as she giggles, forcing me to smack her arm.

"Even I can attest to that," Emma pipes up from her seat on the other side of Georgie. "I'm glad you two are finally together, that way I don't need to deal with him being a cornstalker."

"Cornstalker?" I try not to choke on the sip of my soda I was in the middle of enjoying.

"You know, watching him stalk you through the corn fields," she giggles. "I'm just glad he's using those binoculars to look at birds. Way more soothing."

Georgie and I both cackle, Emma's teasing and humor always bringing levity to any situation. Emma has quickly become another one of my go-to confidants since we met-- thank you, Austin. In fact, if I have my way, I know someone I want to set her up with, but we'll see. Not everyone can get excited about an adult man who dresses up to deliver mail and surprise kids, but you never know. They say everyone has someone out there who is meant for them: I say we all have someone out there whose freak flag matches ours.

"And now he's on a birdwatching kick, thanks to you pointing out the red cardinals in the yard." I toast my cup in the air. "We all need hobbies, don't we?"

"We do," Emma agrees, pointing my way. "Don't forget, right after the game I need you to drop me off for that appointment...is it still okay?"

"Of course," I say. "Is it one of your usual clients?"

"He happens to be in town and asked if I could swing past to check his knee out," she says as she nods, stuffing some popcorn in her mouth.

"Of course, I got you." I put my hand out, managing to clutch Emma's hand as Georgie slaps her on top, adding to our pile. "I'm so lucky I've got you two. I feel like I'm winning at life these days, and it feels nice."

"We're sisters from other misters, right?" Georgie laughs as the three of us toss our hands in the air and cheer.

The announcer's voice booms over the speakers, bringing everyone's attention, including ours, back to the field. My breath catches in my throat as I watch Austin line up, poised and ready. The tension builds, the crowd holds its breath—and then, in an explosion of movement, the play begins.

I can't help but feel my pulse quicken every time he's on the field. It's thrilling, nerve-wracking, and awe-inspiring all at once, knowing that while the whole stadium is cheering, he's out there giving it everything he's got. And somehow, out of all of this, he's mine.

The stadium erupts with noise as the ball snaps, and in an instant, everything moves in slow motion. My eyes are glued to Austin as he takes off down the field, weaving through defenders like they're standing still. The roar of the crowd rises with every step he takes, but all I can hear is the thud of my own heartbeat in my ears.

And then, in one perfect moment, he catches the ball, arms outstretched, and charges toward the end zone. The tension in the stadium is palpable as the final defender closes in, but Austin pivots, breaking free in a burst of speed. The crowd holds a collective breath—then explodes as he crosses into the end zone.

Touchdown.

My heart leaps, and I'm on my feet before I even realize it, screaming his name alongside thousands of others. Austin stands there, arms raised in victory, grinning up at the stands. As his eyes lock with mine, I pat my heart as he blows me a kiss. He looks like he's just conquered the world.

Georgie and Emma jump in the air beside me, their excitement contagious, but all I can think about is how proud I am of him. Not just for the touchdown, but for everything. For staying true to himself. For staying closer to home. For choosing us.

* * *

Austin

After the post game press conference and debrief, I'd hustled as fast as I could to get through a shower and head over to Sinclair Gardens. It's a small venue on the edge of the Charlotte Botanical Gardens that I've rented out for something very special today.

"Hey," Levi's voice breaks me from my spell as he shoves a small jewelry box into the palm of my hand. "You're going to need this."

Grinning, I pull him in for a quick hug. He and mom have been here today getting this spot set up for me. All of this so I can ask Bex the most important question I'm ever going to ask anyone. He'd taken over the duty of setting the table for two in the atrium surrounded by foliage, flowers, and butterflies, and Mom had found the local caterer who is currently getting set up in a kitchen just off the atrium.

The vibration in my pocket pulls my attention to my phone. It's Emma, and she's outside with Bex. It's showtime.

"Okay," I say as I clap my hands together. I look at mom and Levi. "You don't have to go, but you're going to need to hide if you plan on staying."

"Uh uh," my mother says, shaking her head. "We're going to leave you alone for this." She leans in and kisses my cheek. "I'm not going to wish you luck, because she's already a part of our family. I'm just going to say I can't wait to celebrate when she *is* a Porter, because that woman is perfect for you."

As my mom gathers her things and heads to the door, Levi comes up and pulls me into another hug. "You've got this man. Just don't be you and mess it up."

"Ha, you're hilarious!" I shout at his back as he ducks my right hook and jogs out the back door, hot on our mother's heels. I watch as the door behind them closes, fully aware of the door that's behind me beginning to open.

That's right. As one door closed, another one opened, and when I turned to see the love of my life standing there, wearing head-to-toe Cardinals' game day gear and looking a little befuddled, my heart swells inside my chest.

"Austin?" Bex says, holding out hands as she looks at me. "What are you doing here?" She turns and points to Emma, who still sits in the car, idling by the curb. "I thought she had a client..."

"Technically she does," I say, waving to Emma. She throws me a thumbs up and pulls away. "It's me. I'm the client, but I don't need my knee looked at."

Bex scans the room, taking in its beauty, her eyes coming to a rest on the table for two in the middle. "What have you done?"

"I've planned something for you." I slip my hand into hers and walk her over to the table. "Well, it's not only for you. It's for me. For us."

Bex eyes me suspiciously as I pull out her chair. "Austin, what is this?"

I grin, my heart pounding in my chest. "You'll see."

She sits, hesitantly, and I take the seat across from her. The candles on the table flicker, casting soft shadows around us. The room feels intimate, like it's just us in our own little world.

"I wanted to do this right," I begin, my voice steady but my hands slightly trembling. "You deserve that."

She tilts her head, confusion dancing across her face, but there's also curiosity. "Do what?"

I reach into my pocket and pull out a small, velvet box. Bex's eyes widen, her breath catching in her throat.

"Bex," I say, my voice soft, "you came into my life when I didn't know I needed you. I think I had emotionally stopped breathing."

Her eyes sparkle in the candlelight. "What do you mean?"

I grab her hand and hold it tightly in mine. "I think I was in a space where I wasn't allowing myself to feel. I'd cut myself off and was happy sinking down. It was a warm and familiar place by the time you'd come back into my world, and I was happy there."

"Like a pig in…"

"Shush," I say with a laugh, cutting her off as she throws a devilish grin my way. "You've seen me at my worst, and still… you're here. Everyday. Whether you're teaching me something new, jumping in to help my family or the found family you've created around you, or delighting in the world with childlike curiosity or taking on a dog that wasn't yours to begin with-- it doesn't matter what you do, as long as you're beside me. You make me the happiest man in the world. You make me want to be better." I stop, my voice cracking as I take a giant breath of air and then continue. "I can't imagine my life without you in it."

Her eyes glisten, but she stays silent, her lips slightly parted.

"I have made mistakes in my life, big ones, but there is one mistake I'm not going to make with you. I need you to know that I don't want to simply share a night out or a table with you," I continue, my heart racing. "I want to share everything. Forever."

Slowly, I open the box, revealing the ring that my mother helped me pick out for her. Nestled on a pillow of velvet is an emerald-cut diamond in a bespoke setting that I designed, and I can't wait to tell her that part. Her hand flies to her mouth.

"Bex," I say, my voice thick with emotion, "will you marry me?"

For a second, she just stares at the ring, her eyes darting between it and my face. Then, slowly, a smile spreads across her lips.

"You stinker," she whispers, her voice shaky. "Of course, I will."

She leaps into my arms, her lips slanting across mine as she plants a kiss on me that says more than words ever will.

And I feel like I can finally breathe again.

***

Thank you for reading *The Art of Falling in Love with Your Grumpy Neighbor!* If you want to read a BONUS epilogue, from Emma's point of view, and attend the wedding, you can click here to download it now.* You'll even find out what happens to that hedge...

This is the sixth (6th) book in the Sweetkiss Creek Series. All of the books in this series are connected, but don't need to be read in order.

Check out the other books in the Sweetkiss Creek Series here!

If you're reading this book in paperback, you can go to my website www.annekemp.com and sign up for my newsletter. With that, you will get access to the Bonus Epilogue so you don't miss out!
Thank you!

VIP Acknowledgments

I've got some VIPs I must thank. I always say it takes a village to get a book out, and my village keeps growing...

Thank you to **Tara Higgins** for giving Bex her last name: Madden. Very fitting ;)

Thanks goes out to **Heather Johnson** and **Kelli Stowers** for helping me name Emma Rose...and a special shout out to Heather, who has been a great friend of mine for way too long for me to keep track of! She needs a medal...

Thank you to the Sara(h)s in my life: **Sarah Carner,** my PA, and **Sara Kingsley,** who has been my editor for as long as I can remember. Thank you for your support and hard work!

And a shoutout to **Andrea Eason Payne** who is the BEST proofreader an author could ask for. Your attention to the finest details blows me away!

YOU GUYS ARE THE BEST!!

Acknowledgments

Oh boy...book six in the Sweetkiss Creek series is here and I'd always planned to say goodbye to the town at this point. To wrap it up because the stories would have been told, and we would have gotten to know the folks we needed to. Right?

The past few weeks as I've finished this book, I've found myself to be melancholy. Dragging my feet when it came to getting this book done. Questioning the next step, but wondering why I'm feeling this way.

Then it hit me: I'm not ready. I'm not ready to leave Sweetkiss Creek. Not yet.

So, there will be a seventh book in this series and it will be out in 2025 because **The Art of Falling in Love with Your Billionaire Boss** is a THING, you guys! ;)

Thank you for being with me and the folks in this small town for our journey so far--and happy reading!

Author's Note

This book has a storyline I've been wanting to write about for a while now.

No, it's not the grumpy nor the sunshine. It's not the warring neighbors and it's not the football.

It's about having Graves' disease--which I have and have been living with since 2011.

My journey with Graves' disease is not going to be like anyone else's. When I first found out I had it, I learned very quickly that what I was dealing with wasn't going to mimic another person who was dealing with hyperthyroid.

I'm not going to go into the details of my autoimmune origin story, but I wanted to share with you that it took ME pushing my own cart uphill to get the diagnosis. That doctors were getting it wrong, because they are human, so I was staying on top of MY needs.

I went through almost a year of misdiagnosis before I found my team of people who helped me get to the bottom of why my health was suddenly failing. And then, I made the active choice to fully change my life so I could fight what was happening to my body.

If you have a thyroid issue or disease, maybe you have hyperthyroid like I do, or hypothyroid. It could be Graves' disease or Hashimoto's. Whatever it is, FIND your support team. Get them behind you and then do what you need to do to put yourself first. Look for positive resources where you can learn about what you're dealing with.

And also know that I get it. I see you.

We've got this.

Anne xo

About the Author

Anne Kemp is an author of romantic comedies,
sweet contemporary romance, and chick lit.
She loves reading (and does it ridiculously fast, too!), gluten-free baking
(because everyone needs a hobby that makes them crazy), and
finding time to binge-watch her favorite shows. She grew up in
Maryland but made Los Angeles her home until she
encountered her own real-life meet-cute at a friend's wedding
where she ended up married to one of the groomsmen.
For real.

Anne now lives on the Kapiti Coast in New Zealand, and even
though she was married at Mt. Doom, no...she doesn't have a
Hobbit. However, she and her husband do have a terrier
named George Clooney and a rescue pup named Charlie.
When she's not writing, she's usually with them taking a long
walk on the river by their home.

Also by Anne Kemp

Sweetkiss Creek Series

Welcome to Sweetkiss Creek, where the locals are nosy, the dogs are pushy, and love could be just around the corner...

The Sweetkiss Creek series are closed door rom coms, filled with close friendships, swoony kisses, and lots of laughs!

The Art of Falling in Love with Your Best Friend

Dylan and Reid's story

friends-to-lovers

The Art of Falling in Love with Your Enemy

Etta and Zac's story

enemies to lovers + grumpy sunshine

The Art of Falling in Love with the Movie Star

Amelia and Spencer's Christmas story

second chance celebrity romance

The Art of Falling in Love with Your Brother's Best Friend

Riley and Jake's story

enemies to lovers + ice hockey star

The Art of Falling in Love with Your Fake Fiancé

Georgie and Levi's story

the bookstore owner + the NFL star

The Art of Falling in Love with Your Grumpy Neighbor

Bex and Austin's story

Thank you for reading!

Love in Lake Lorelei Series

Ahhh...Lake Lorelei, the small town down the road from Sweetkiss Creek. These sweet romcoms are sizzling with chemistry and bringing you all the feels.

Get to know this small town, its locals and, most importantly, the Lake Lorelei Fire Department!

Sweet Summer Nights (Book 1)

Freya and Wyatt's story

The Sweet Spot (Book 2)

Ari and Carter's story

When Sparks Fly (Book 3)

Maisey and Jack's story

The Abby George Series

The Abby George books are closed-door, Chick lit comedies with a lil' sass, a touch of sarcasm, and some innuendo, but guaranteed to have you laughing out loud as you fall in love!

Rum Punch Regrets

Gotta Go To Come Back

Sugar City Secrets

Caribbean Romance Novella

Part of the Abby George world but can be read as a stand alone story.

This book is a sweet and clean closed door

romantic comedy.

Second Chance for Christmas

Stay up-to-date on new releases, get special bonus content, and special promotions when you sign up for

Anne's newsletter.

*If you're reading this book in paperback, you can go to my website www.annekemp.com and sign up for my newsletter so you don't miss out!

Made in the USA
Middletown, DE
08 October 2024